I0784769

ED J. THOMPSON

Out of Darkness

Ed J. Thompson

Fiction and Literature: Inspirational Christian mystery and suspense

ISBN:978-1-968792-58-9

For Mom

When Jesus spoke again to the people, he said, "I am the light
    of the world. Whoever follows me will never walk in
    darkness, but will have the light of life."
    John 8:12 (NIV)

For our struggle is not against flesh and blood, but against the
    rulers, against the authorities, against the
powers of this dark
            world and against the spiritual forces of
        evil in the heavenly realms. Therefore, put
        on the full armor of God, so that when the
        day of evil comes, you may be able to stand
        your ground, and after you have done
        everything, to stand.
            Ephesians 6:12-13 (NIV)

    We must accept finite disappointment
    but never lose infinite hope.
    Martin Luther King, Jr.

Chapter 1

Oftentimes, those of us who grew up poor in the American inner city felt like we didn't matter or have any control over our lives. It's like a dark storm cloud was always hovering above, that you can only escape or ignore for so long. Arguably, the road to clearer skies was paved by more than elite athleticism, fame or fortune, or even education, because none of those things can bring about true healing of the soul.

Rather, it's a genuine knowing in the secret place in the corner of your heart and mind that you were born to reign in this life. That is, no matter what happens, or how broken or sad we feel, we are all created in the image of God Himself… of immeasurable worth! My life changed when my purpose for living changed. That's when I first began to put my trust in the Lord and make my life a living testimony.

I was devastated when my mother suddenly died a month before my wedding. It felt like I got stabbed again… but this time in the heart. She died in her sleep from heart failure. She was only 46 years old.

She never really took care of herself, a little too much partying and alcohol, not enough sunlight. I seriously doubted that she ever went to see a doctor for anything, except maybe early on when she was pregnant. The autopsy revealed that she had an enlarged heart, which she most likely never knew she had. She lived alone and died several days before she was discovered by a neighbor.

I spoke to her on the phone a week before her passing. We had recently gotten into the habit of talking every week or so. None of our conversations lasted that long, maybe 15 or 20 minutes. All she talked about the last time we spoke was how much she was looking forward to seeing me get married. She bought a new dress for the occasion. She said that it was the first dress she had owned since she was a little girl. It was blue and white with ruffles. We buried her in it.

I was haunted by all of my harsh judgments about her that I had held close to my heart for so long. I was broken by the guilt and shame, crushed by my own silent curses. After everything that we had been through, we were just beginning to find true peace in our relationship. I had fully embraced the possibilities, and I believed that God was going to finish the miracles that he had started in us both.

It's funny how the course of one's life can drastically change in a moment. I have heard quite a few believers say that that's exactly what happened to them in the moment that they first gave their lives to Jesus. Some talked about how on that day they instantly lost the taste for many of their vices— such as cigarettes, alcohol, and drugs— and they were able to put some or all of these bad habits behind them for good.

I have always envied those people a little because I definitely was not the recipient of that kind of miracle. I was basically still the same guy on the outside after I was saved as I was before my conversion. The only difference was that after realizing that God is real, I suddenly began to hunger and thirst in my heart to really know Him and to otherwise be pleasing to Him.

In essence, there were no shortcuts for me. Clearly, I needed to walk some things out regardless of how long it took and how painful that process might be. Nobody told me that it would be easy, but it was often much harder than I thought it would be. My faith was tested by fire many times over the years; both my body and mind were often scorched and seared.

When my mother died, I knew in my heart that I would never be the same again. I kept thinking about what might have been and about all of the missed opportunities and wasted time. Our social class and ethnicity, along with a healthy dose of victim mentality, had blinded us both, which prevented us from being able to get out of our own way and find the love and acceptance that we both so desperately craved.

I hated that I never told her that I loved her, but I honestly don't know if I ever really did love her, at least not the way that a good son is supposed to love his mother. Unbridled anger is an evil and powerful force. But I knew that deep down I always wanted to love her— if that counts for something. Having to accept that this was the absolute end for us and that there was no going back or rewriting our ending was absolutely suffocating. The pain of regret is particularly bitter and unrelenting.

I never cried so much in my life as I did in the days surrounding the funeral. Emotions erupted in me like hot lava and ash from a volcano, which meant that they burned in my soul too. This was new territory for me in that I had always been so guarded and measured publicly. Suddenly, everyone could see that it was all for show. I was embarrassed, too.

I wasn't really in any position to console my grandmother, who had completely shut down emotionally. However, unlike me, she never shed a tear that I saw. She was a tough woman, but I knew that she was suffering as well. She disappeared into herself and was only present when she absolutely needed to be. No doubt, her tortured past with my mother was weighing heavily on her, too.

But I knew that I couldn't be the one to save her, not this time. Her issues with her daughter were different than mine. It was like we were both sinking in the same swamp of quicksand, so we were unable to reach out to each other for a helping hand. We needed to figure this one out for ourselves. Neither one of us was at risk of actually drowning, even though it was a scary and uneasy feeling just the same.

All kinds of people showed up at the funeral home, including my future in-laws and my former colleagues from the public defender's office. I really appreciated the support. Both my sisters were there, too, from Buffalo, and they brought their children with them, all of whom I met for the first time. Sadly, they never knew their grandmother either.

There was also a rather large contingency of people who knew my mother from the streets and the underbelly of the city of Utica. I had never met most of them before, but they acted like they knew me. Unexpectedly, I was perceived by everyone as the next of kin and chief mourner. I felt like neither one.

I kept telling myself to keep everything in perspective… and to take deep breaths. After all, I still had Carla, my reason for breathing. Needless to say, I loved Carla so much that it scared me, and nothing else really mattered to me as much as she did. So, I knew without a doubt that I would eventually heal from this loss too, even if it hurt like hell in the process.

I didn't speak at all at the short service. My sister Tasha spoke a few words on behalf of our family— something about how our mother loved to have a good time with friends and had a beautiful smile. Sitting there, I racked my brain for something more profound to say, but I honestly couldn't think of anything, which only added to my shame.

Ultimately, the ties of my past that held me bound for so long were, in a very real sense, buried in the grave with my mother. I suddenly realized that even if she had lived to a ripe old age, and our relationship had blossomed into something great over time, she still would have symbolized, in part, the demonic presence that kept me oppressed and lost in darkness, with almost everyone else I knew growing up poor and Black in the city.

Chapter 2

It still felt strange whenever someone told me that Pastor Justin wanted to talk to me. I couldn't help but wonder if I was in trouble for something. Most of the people in our church seemed to hold him and Pastor Marlene, his wife, in almost god-like esteem. I was never one of them. Even before we started hanging out a little bit and became friends, I saw him as just a regular guy who just happened to also be my pastor.

I'm pretty sure that that was one of the reasons that Pastor Justin liked me so much. He felt that he could be himself around me. We bonded while I was recovering from my leg injury. He started calling me on the phone a lot, and we just hit it off. We both liked to joke around and neither one of us was addicted to sports or popular culture. I wasn't looking to become friends with him, but for some reason, he pursued me in that way.

"Sam, might we have a word in private?" Pastor Justin whispered in my ear shortly after the benediction one Sunday.

"Yeah, sure," I replied and followed him out of the main sanctuary.

When we got to his office, he stepped aside so that I could get by and immediately shut the door behind us. The top of his desk was cluttered with papers and books, the remnant of all of his intense preparation. He wasn't just a gifted speaker, but he also put in the work. It was all worth the effort, and his sermon today, entitled "Out of Darkness," was excellent. I really enjoyed it.

"Sam, have a seat," he said.

"*Darkness in the Wilderness*" was the title of one of the books on his desk. I couldn't see the author's name from where I was sitting.

Pastor took off his dark blue suit jacket and hung it behind the door. He took in a deep breath and exhaled loudly as he sat down behind the desk. He immediately loosened his tie and unbuttoned the top button on his shirt.

"What's up?" I asked.

"Uh… I don't really want to have to talk about this, but you are the only one whom I trust enough to mention it to," he offered.

"Okay."

"I received a rather unpleasant phone call yesterday from a man whose wife I have been counseling. He was very angry, and he accused me of having an affair with her. He threatened to go public with this accusation if I didn't cut it off with her immediately."

"Are you?" I asked.

He was startled.

"What? Having an affair with his wife?"

"Yes, are you?" I repeated.

"No, of course not! I would never do such a thing!"

"Then why does he think that you are?"

"I don't know."

"You don't have any idea?"

"No, I don't," he objected. "How would I know that?"

"I'm just asking the question," I said and laughed to myself.

"Do you really think that is something that I would do?" he asked.

"How are you counseling her?" I redirected his focus.

"We met a couple of times here in my office during regular business hours."

"Alone?" I questioned. "You met with her alone?"

"Yes," he answered, and quickly averted his eyes. "You think that was a mistake?"

I looked at him with some skepticism as I digested the scenario fully.

"I meet with most people alone," he defended. "There's nothing unusual about that."

"What are you counseling her for?" I quizzed.

"They are having marital problems," he disclosed. "Now that I think about it, that's probably what this is all about. I don't think that he likes some of the things that I have told her to do. It seems that he's quite the philanderer himself. He's also abusive."

"Are they members here?"

"She's been coming for about a year, I'd say. She comes by herself. I've never met him."

"You never met with the two of them together?"

Pastor Justin shook his head.

"He's not interested in counseling," he stated. "He's not a believer."

"I see," I replied.

Pastor looked tired around the eyes. He pressed his thin lips together and rubbed

his eyes with his right hand as he leaned forward on the desk. His dark curly hair was still perfectly in place. I knew him well enough to know that he was really tired. Good thing that Sunday afternoons were created for resting.

"Did you tell Pastor Marlene about this threatening phone call?" I inquired further.

"No, I didn't."

"Why not?"

"I wanted to talk to you first."

I slowly sat up straight in my chair.

"So, Pastor, how can I help you with all of this? What can I do?"

"I just wanted some advice," he asserted. "I know how this looks, and I don't want to do anything to make matters worse."

"Well, I think you need to tell your wife right away."

"Okay."

"Are you worried about doing that?" I pressed.

"No, I wasn't planning on keeping this from her."

"And I also think that you should cut off all contact with this woman immediately. You don't know what she's been telling her husband."

"Right."

"Just make your life a little easier," I remarked.

"Can he try to sue me for something?" Pastor wondered.

"Possibly, but I think it's more likely that he would just try to spread rumors and ruin your reputation."

"That could really destroy everything we've started here," he articulated and let out a heavy sigh.

"Yes, I guess he certainly could cause some real problems for you," I conceded. "But it sounds to me that he is just trying to scare you."

"Can I sue him if he follows through in some way?"

"Yes, but most of the damage would already have been done," I maintained. "It's hard to put the genie back in the bottle."

"So, there's nothing that I can do now to stop him from spreading these false accusations against us?" Pastor demanded.

"Against *you*," I corrected.

"That's what I meant."

"Probably not," I said. "Not if that's something he really wants to do."

"Then he wins," Pastor concluded.

"Keep in mind that he would also be throwing his wife under the bus, too, if he went public with his claims," I articulated. "And himself too, I might add. No man wants the whole world to know that his wife has turned to another man, even if that man is a minister. No, it sounds like he just wants you to stop meeting with her."

"That way, he can continue beating her and treating her like crap!" Pastor protested.

"There are other people she can counsel with besides you," I set forth.

"I know there are."

"You should probably consider telling your overseers, too, what is going on," I advised.

His eyes opened wide.

"What? You mean, you think I should tell our board of elders? Can't we wait to see what happens?"

"Don't you think that this is something that they might want to know?" I argued.

"Maybe, but you don't know them," he replied. "They are going to make this bigger than what it really needs to be."

"How so?"

"I don't know exactly, but this won't sit well with them," he indicated. "I'm already embarrassed enough."

"I get that, but I wouldn't wait too much longer because the longer you wait, the more it looks like you have something to hide," I reflected. "They might want your insurance carrier to know."

"But might this all just blow over once this guy calms down and comes to his senses? I never touched Lacey."

"*Lacey*?" I asked.

"Yes, Lacey Stanton."

"The young blonde woman on the worship team?" I inquired. "Isn't her name Lacey?"

"Yes, that's her."

"You're kidding!" I exclaimed.

"No, why?"

"Nothing, it's just that she looks like she could be in the movies," I commented. "I didn't know she was married."

"Does it matter how she looks?"

"No, not at all," I answered and smirked. "It's just that I get now why her husband might be the jealous type."

"Is that because you're the jealous type too?" he challenged.

"I don't know what I am," I hedged. "But even God himself is jealous, right? It's an honest emotion."

"Are you defending this guy for threatening me?"

"Not at all," I resisted. "I'm just saying that I know what

it's like to be with a really attractive woman. It can mess with your head."

"I'm not having an affair with Lacey," Pastor stated emphatically.

"You said that already," I replied.

"Do you believe me?"

A look of desperation came over him, and he stared at me intently.

"I don't think it matters what I believe," I asserted.

"It matters to me… I really respect you, and I want to know what you think."

The office door suddenly swung open, and Pastor Marlene walked in. She was tall, thin, and attractive. She had shoulder-length blonde hair with short bangs. She was wearing a conservative dark blue boat-neck dress and black square-toe pumps. I could smell her perfume, which was something floral.

"Oh, I'm sorry!" she exclaimed. "I didn't know that there was anybody in here with you. Hi Sam."

"Hi," I answered.

"How's Carla?"

"She's good," I replied. "She's on complete bedrest, so she's going a little stir crazy, I think."

"Poor dear! How much longer does she have?"

"She's 20 weeks, so we are halfway there, unless they decide to induce her," I disclosed. "But the doctor is mostly concerned about her blood pressure, which is really high and affecting her. So, they are watching her closely."

"Please tell her that I asked about her and that I'm going to call her," she requested.

"I will."

"Do you guys need anything?" she solicited.

"Not really. Carla's mom and sister are here a lot. They pretty much have everything covered. I feel like I'm in the way most of the time."

"You're not in the way," she encouraged. "Husbands play a bigger role in this than you guys know. She needs your strength. Justin was great when I was pregnant."

"I know," I relented. "It's just there's so much going on."

"Yeah, I get that, but please don't hesitate to let us know if there is anything that we can do to help out," she graciously offered.

"Thank you," I replied. "I appreciate that." "Honey, we have to head out soon," she told her husband. "JR has a baseball game, and we still need to figure out something for dinner."

"Okay," Pastor Justin replied. "Can you just give Sam and me another minute?"

"I'll go gather up the boys," she said, and walked out and closed the door.

"So, tell me what you really think?" Pastor insisted.

"I think it's too early to know anything," I answered. "I know that it's hard, but we just have to wait and see what happens. It could all blow over like you say. The ball isn't really in your court."

"What if it doesn't?" Pastor pressed.

"Then we adjust accordingly," I said. "As you know, scandals in the church aren't anything new. I think the most important thing is to protect the congregation. We don't want people to get hurt or lose heart."

"No, I don't want that," he whispered. "Our people are

the salt of the earth."

"So, go home and try not to worry."

"Okay, but you believe me when I tell you that I'm not having an affair with Lacey?"

His eyes begged for my support.

I only hesitated slightly.

"You're my pastor," I spoke. "I believe what you tell me."

— • ● • —

I tried not to make too much noise as I opened the side door off the garage and walked into the kitchen. I didn't want to wake Carla. She slept a lot these days. Our lives have changed immensely in the last year and a half. We got married, bought a house, and found out that we were expecting twins, not to mention my new job at the law firm. It was quite the whirlwind, to say the least. I could hardly believe that this was now my life.

Without a doubt, the scariest part was buying the house. I signed my name to a 30-year mortgage, and I was just 30 years old. I broke out in a sweat right there at the attorney's office as I struggled to gather myself. It felt like I was signing my life away. Carla laughed at me.

It was a four-bedroom colonial in a quiet neighborhood that we jokingly referred to as *the white house*." Carla's mom found it for us, and her father co-signed on the mortgage. I never dreamed that I would ever live in a house this nice. I was starting to believe that anything was possible for us.

"What are you doing?" I asked as I opened the door and

turned the sharp corner into the kitchen and discovered her standing there.

"What does it look like?" Carla replied. "I'm making your lunch."

"You're supposed to be resting," I argued.

"I'm tired of resting."

"I can make my own lunch," I stated.

"I'm just pregnant, Sam. I'm not dying," she protested. "Teenagers do it every day."

"You're not a teenager," I argued. "You know the doctor is worried about your blood pressure. How's your headache?"

"I don't have one."

"Good."

"Do you want tomatoes on your grilled cheese?"

"I want you to start listening," I responded.

"Sam, I already told you I'm fine. I should have gone to church with you."

"Do you want me to call your mother?"

"You better not call her!" she threatened. "It's bad enough that she's here all the time. These people are driving me out of my mind."

I sat down at the kitchen table. The kitchen was the only room in the house that was somewhat organized. There were boxes piled up in all the other rooms, even though we moved in two months ago. The den was covered with open wedding gifts that Carla wouldn't let anyone put away. She was being more than a little difficult.

"Look, I know it's not easy for you," I said. "But you're almost there."

"I'm getting nervous about the nursery," she blurted

out.

"The nursery? Why?"

"I want to decorate it myself."

"No way."

"I'll be careful."

"No, you won't," I resisted. "It's too risky."

"It's really not that big of a deal."

"Let your mother and your sister help you with that."

"You don't understand," she objected. "I don't want their help. This is an important part of it for me. This is supposed to be *my* time."

She put a plate holding my sandwich and a glass of diet cola down in front of me.

"I'm sorry, but I don't know what to tell you," I submitted. "You have to think about the babies."

"I am thinking about them."

I just looked at her. She was big pregnant. But she was all stomach. Her face was unaffected. I didn't think it was possible, but she was more beautiful than ever.

"You're still in charge of everything here," I said. "Just be the team leader and boss them around the way you do me. We already know that you're really good at doing that."

"I don't boss you around," she maintained. "It's not my fault that you need so much help."

"Excuse me?" I reacted.

"Are you gonna eat?" she asked.

"Yes, thank you."

"You want coffee?"

"Yes, please."

"So, you really think I can do this, huh?"

Her eyes got big. I felt the full force of her words, which

were saturated with simmering apprehension and lingering self-doubt.

"I know you can," I whispered with a reassuring smile. "Piece of cake for my girl!"

She looked deep into my eyes as I held strong to my resolve.

"Hmm," she remarked before pivoting and walking away.

Chapter 3

My adjustment from the public defender's office to being an associate at McMann & Tatum LLC wasn't necessarily a smooth one. I was used to a big office with a lot of people running around all the time and hearing the phones ringing off the hook all day. This was almost too quiet. There were only four attorneys, including me, one paralegal, and a receptionist. I don't exactly know why, but everything seemed bigger and darker. The days seem to drag, which was one of the things that I was worried most about before I accepted their offer to join them.

Initially, I was secretly convinced that I had made a big mistake. I felt like a fish out of water. They had nothing for me to do. They billed clients by the hour, and I had no real prospects in sight. They paid me a salary that was more than twice as much as I made at the public defender's office and gave me a big office with a nice view of downtown Utica. I clearly had moved up in the world.

However, I felt self-imposed pressure to start producing from my first day in the office. Tony DiLauro, the partner who recruited me, kept telling me to relax about the work, but I was more than a little anxious. The truth is that in my head, I couldn't see how this could work out.

All I did in those first few weeks was handle a few speeding tickets and do research for Jake Russo, the other associate. I liked Jake. He was tall and thin with sandy-brown hair and round-framed glasses. He was only a few years older than me, and he represented a lot of banks. I didn't know anything about business or commercial law, and frankly, none of it interested me. But he knew a lot of people, and he could hopefully help me land a few clients of my own, people who needed a trial attorney.

My first real case actually came from Jake. Zoe Carter, a bank manager's daughter, was fired from her job at an insurance company, and she claimed that the termination was the result of her refusal to give in to her boss's sexual advances. She said that he kept trying to put his hands up her shirt. Her father was outraged, and he was behind the charge to sue the insurance company and the manager. I didn't know much about sexual harassment or wrongful termination cases, but I was desperate for something interesting to do.

I first met Zoe when she came to the office with both her parents, who were an interracial couple. Joe, her father, was a short, pudgy, middle-aged white man. Her mother, Pauline, was tall and slim with short hair and dark skin. Zoe didn't look anything like either of her parents, but rather was a mixture of the two. She was light-skinned with long curly brown hair and light hazel eyes. Objectively, she was very attractive. She could probably pass for a nonblack woman if she were so inclined.

"Zoe, how old are you?" I asked

"I'm 24."

"Do you still live with your parents?"

"No, I live in an apartment in New Hartford."

"How far did you go in school?"

"I have an associate's degree from community college, MVCC."

"What was your major?"

"Social work."

"How long did you work at Longley?"

"A little over a year."

"What did you do there?"

"I was a claims adjuster."

"How many people worked there?"

"There were four of us."

"What are their names?"

"Cody Sinner, Mark Volpe …and Bob Wells."

"You were the only woman?"

"Yes."

"And Bob Wells was your supervisor?"

"Yeah, basically... I mean, he has been there the longest. We all pretty much did the same work, though."

"When did you start having problems with him?"

"Um, I'd say pretty much from the beginning. First, he started complimenting me all the time. He kept telling me how he liked my outfit or the way I smelled. Then he started trying to touch me … like on my shoulder and my arm?"

"How did you respond to his touching you?"

"I tried to ignore it at first, but then I just started backing up every time he put his hands on me."

"What did he do when you backed up?"

"Sometimes he just laughed," she indicated. "Other times, he just walked away. He also liked to adjust himself in front of me."

"How often did he do these things? I mean… try to touch you."

"A lot," she said. "It wasn't like every day, you know, but he did it whenever he could."

"Did you complain to anyone?"

"I told Cody and Mark."

"Did they do anything to help you?"

"Mark said he told Bob to cut it out."

"But Bob continued?" I asked.

"Yeah, he did," she replied. "I just kept my distance from him. Then he cornered me one night when we were alone in the office. He tried to put his hand up the side of my blouse, and I pushed him away hard. After that, he started picking on me and being really critical of everything I did. He started talking bad about me to Cody and Mark. I couldn't take it anymore, and I called central office and reported him."

"Where is the central office?"

"It's in Albany."

"Did they do anything?" I wondered.

"They sent a woman from Albany to talk to me, and they fired me a week later."

"What did you tell her?"

"Just what I just told you," She answered. "That Bob wouldn't let up, you know. I told her that I didn't want to get him in trouble or anything. I just wanted it to stop."

"Do you remember her name by chance?"

"Aw…Cathy something," she replied. "I can't remember the last name."

"Did they say why they fired you?"

"They just said that my services were no longer needed."

"Did they give you anything in writing?"

"Just this notice of termination."

She took a piece of paper out of her bag and handed it to me. I looked at it briefly.

"Can they fire her just like that?" Joe Carter interjected.

"Probably not," I answered.

"What do you mean?" he probed. "I always thought there had to be a lawful reason to fire people. At the bank, we are really careful about doing that sort of thing."

"This notice doesn't say anything," I commented. "My guess is that the company is going to come up with some pretense for doing what they did?"

"Like what?" asked Mr. Carter.

" Zoe, have you ever received any criticism of your work," I delved deeper. "Anything official like a counseling memo or bad performance reviews?"

"No, I haven't."

"Well, they are never going to admit that they fired you because you complained about your supervisor's behavior," I stated. "If you want to challenge this, you need to know that it won't be easy. People generally play dirty when backed into a corner."

"Doesn't matter," Mr. Carter said. "I want them to pay for what they did."

"Zoe?" I asked.

"What will they do?" she wondered.

"They are going to try to ruin your reputation," I suspected. "Can you handle that?"

I thought I saw fear in her eyes. I definitely saw her

anguish.

"Can't we just get them to pay a settlement or something?" she questioned. "I don't want to work there anymore anyway."

"Probably not," I advised. "At least not right away. They have to put up a fight."

Zoe looked at her mother, and the two had a rapid nonverbal exchange of sentiment that I saw clearly. I don't think that her father was aware.

Her mother suddenly spoke up.

"When you say that they are going to try to ruin my daughter's reputation, can they really talk in court about personal things that have absolutely nothing to do with whether that lecher groped her repeatedly?"

"Hard to say," I admitted. "They will investigate your past – prior relationships and boyfriends — and try to show that you shouldn't be believed."

"I see," Mrs. Carter responded.

I could see the wheels turning in her head.

"Do you have any other questions?"

There was silence.

"Okay, folks," I began. "You don't have to decide anything right now. This consultation today is free of charge. If you decide that you do want to retain this firm to represent you… to sue this insurance company on your behalf, then you can let us know. I have to get the approval of the partners here to move forward. Either way, it was very nice meeting you all."

"Thank you," they each responded together and stood.

"I'll be here, too, if you have any other questions," I volunteered. "Please feel free to call me at any time."

"Thank you, Mr. Hicks," Zoe said again.

"And for what it's worth," I added. "Zoe, I believe what you say happened to you, and I'm really sorry that you had to experience that."

"Thank you," she uttered.

I led them to the door and walked slowly back to my office. I felt a little anxious because I really wanted this case. But I honestly wasn't sure that I was the best choice for them. I only took one course in law school in employment law, and I didn't remember much about the subject matter. There were a few firms in Utica that specialized in it. I could easily find myself outmatched and over my head.

But there was something about Zoe that spoke to me. I wasn't exactly sure what it was. She seemed sad in her soul My sense was that she never would have come to see me in the first place if her father hadn't forced her into it.

If she were one of my clients at the public defender's office, I would have insisted on speaking to her alone, without anyone else in the room. But this was different because her parents would probably be the ones paying our legal fees. It's hard to kick the people out of the room who were paying your fees.

Truthfully, I was very excited at the prospect of championing the underdog again. That probably was my greatest strength both as a lawyer and as a Christian. I don't think that any true believer can simply turn a blind eye to the pain and injustice in the world. Jesus certainly didn't.

I decided not to get my hopes up. There was no way of knowing what this family was going to do. There is always a risk associated with deciding to sue somebody because, typically, there are no guarantees that you will prevail. It's a lot of time, energy, and money to expend upfront — not to mention the embarrassment from opening oneself up to public scrutiny.

I had two new DWI cases on my desk, which I could do in my sleep. Fortunately, there was plenty more where they came from, so I wasn't just sitting at my desk all day looking at the walls. They were just going to have to do for now because they were the only quasi-criminal cases that the firm was willing to let me take.

The fact is that there wasn't any real money in criminal defense work outside of the rare cases where some wealthy doctor is indicted for murdering his wife, or something equally as scandalous. Most of the people charged with crimes in this county are poor, which means that they can no longer afford me. Seemingly, those days were over for me.

Chapter 4

Pastor Justin called me at work and asked if we could get together. For some reason, he was always the one who initiated our meetings. I almost never called him, even though I enjoyed his company. I asked him if something was wrong, but he didn't want to get into it on the phone. We made plans to meet at the diner we both liked which was located close to the church.

I arrived first and quickly found a table in the rear. There was a guy sitting at the counter talking to the waitress as I walked past. I sat there alone for about five minutes until she came to take my order. I liked the coffee there, which was the only thing I typically wanted. I inhaled my first cup before Pastor got there.

He worked at the post office, and he was wearing his light blue postal shirt. Something about seeing him dressed like that always made me want to laugh. He once told me that his hope was that one day he wouldn't have to work outside of the church. But he didn't really mind working the window at the local post office. He knew everybody, and about five or six of his co-workers were members of his church. It was apparently a great place to meet people.

"Sorry, I'm late," he said. "I had to take JR to practice, and he forgot his cleats at home, so I had to double-back."

"No problem."

"How's Carla?"

"She's all right."

The waitress appeared and brought a cup for Pastor and gave me a refill.

"How are you, Sam?"

"I'm hanging in there," I answered. "We're just taking it one day at a time."

"Well, you know the whole church is holding you guys up in prayer."

"I know," I acknowledged. "What's going on with you?"

"I wanted to talk to you about Lacey again."

His face contorted.

"What about her?" I asked.

"I met with her."

"In person?"

"Yes."

"I thought we agreed that you should stay away from her."

"I know, but I had to meet with her so I could tell her why I couldn't counsel her anymore."

"How'd it go?"

"Not good. She was very upset."

"How so?"

"She said her husband is bluffing…. That he's just trying to control her."

"Maybe he is, but you can't take the chance," I expressed.

"I was wondering …I was thinking that maybe we could still meet over the phone or something? What do you think?"

"What does Pastor Marlene think?"

"I haven't told her yet."

I chuckled to myself.

"What?" Pastor asked.

"You know what," I asserted.

"No, I don't," Pastor replied. "I just feel sorry for Lacey. She's a good person who grew up in foster care with no family of her own and who is really in a bad place living with a man who is trying to crush her spirit every day. I'd like to help her if I can."

"What about your wife?"

"What about her?"

"She's Lacey's pastor, too," I contended. "Let her counsel Lacey."

"It's not the same," he stated.

"Why not?"

"Because Marlene doesn't know Lacey."

"Neither do you," I suggested. "You said that you only met with her a few times. Sounds to me like you might be getting in too deep."

"No, I don't think that I am," Pastor refuted. "I just feel like I can help her get out of this mess she's in. And she trusts me."

"Well, Pastor, I don't really know… I just don't think that it's a good idea for you to continue to meet with her in any kind of way. It's too easy for you to get caught up in something that you can't control and lose everything."

"*Everything?*"

"Yes, *everything*," I insisted. "I know you care about

your reputation, but jealousy and love makes people do things that they wouldn't ordinarily do."

"He doesn't love Lacey," he maintained.

"How do you know?" I questioned. "Did you ask him?"

"I know what Lacey told me."

"Exactly, not good enough," I deflected. "You don't have any idea who you are dealing with. This guy could be a psychopath for all you know. He already gave you a strong warning. You'd be wise to walk away, I tell you."

Pastor slowly lifted his cup to his mouth, took a sip of his coffee, and looked at me in earnest.

"I'm sorry," I expressed.

"You don't understand," he finally said. "I'm her pastor. It's hard to see one of the sheep in your flock in pain."

"…No, I get that," I offered. "But you don't really have a choice in my opinion."

———•●•———

My take was that Pastor was much more naïve than I was when it came to the ways of the world. I never would have guessed that that would have been the case. He was such a gifted teacher and student of the Bible that it was easy to just assume that he was wise in every area of life. But that really wasn't true.

Unlike Pastor, I was raised in the inner city of Utica in utter poverty, where dysfunction was the norm. Moreover, in my four years at the public defender's office, I had seen the unmasked face of evil several times, actually being locked alone in a jail cell with one of his hosts on more than one occasion. As a result, I was a jaded man cloaked in realism and a healthy dose of skepticism.

Indeed, Jesus said that we should be as wise as serpents, not like innocent sheep among wolves. Life had trained me to always be on guard. I thought Pastor leaned too much toward the opposite spectrum— having dove like innocence. I found that finding the right balance is the key.

In my mind, I always made a clear distinction between whether I was relating to him as a friend or as my pastor at any particular time. I didn't want to cross any lines with him, and I always wanted to be respectful. He told me once that he missed having friends and buddies who treated him like he was just one of the guys. I felt that I could be both his friend and one of his members, but the truth is that I definitely needed a pastor more than I needed a friend— no doubt about it.

To be clear, I didn't have any desire to play a leadership role in the church. I was still new to the things of God, and I felt strongly that I needed to be discipled as much as anyone. I agreed to help Elder Dick with the monthly men's meeting, but I really wasn't ready to teach Sunday School to kids or lead some other kind of group. There were just so many things that I still needed to learn.

— • ● • —

I found that a part of me really missed being in the public defender's office. I didn't, however, miss the low pay and poor working conditions or being treated like I wasn't a real lawyer worthy of respect. Although the work there was often grueling and intense, I discovered that I was a bit of a rebel in need of a cause.

It wasn't a secret that I enjoyed the challenge of a good fight, and I seriously doubted that I would ever get the same kind of rush again from my work, which in the end, was a rather small price to pay for a better life for my family and me. I told myself that it was time for me to grow up and be a man about it.

Pastor Justin taught a lot about the need for every Christian to be a good steward of the gifts of God in our lives. He didn't just mean our money or material possessions, but also our time and our talents. I felt strongly that I needed to do something meaningful with my life that made a real difference for other people without getting anything back.

Defending poor and indigent people caught up in the legal system is an important and vital role in American society. Now that I had put the public defender's office behind me, I needed to find a substitute that gave me the same kind of personal satisfaction. In the end, we are all called to serve humanity.

Chapter 5

I woke up to the sound of running water. Carla was in the shower. The clock read 7:33 a.m. It was Sunday, and I didn't have to get up for another hour and so I rolled over onto my stomach and put my face in my pillow until I heard her walking about.

"What are you doing?" I inquired.

"What does it look like?"

"I don't know."

"I'm getting ready for church."

"What?" I reacted. "You're not going to church?"

"Yes, I am," she contended.

"No, you're not."

"You can't hold me hostage here," she maintained.

I laughed.

"What's so funny?" she questioned.

"Listen, Harriet Tubman," I joked. "I thought we decided that…"

"No, you all decided for me," Carla argued. "But not today! So, either you take me with you, or I will drive myself. Those are your choices."

"I don't understand why you are being so difficult," I

countered and sat up in bed. "You heard what the doctor said."

"I'm not being difficult," she rebuked. "I just want to go to church with my husband. Is that such a bad thing? I'm not a child. I know what's best for me and what I can and cannot do!"

"I'm not sure you do."

"What's that supposed to mean?" she snapped. "You think that because I'm pregnant that I have suddenly lost my mind?"

"I'm just asking you to be reasonable."

"And I'm asking you to trust me," she came back.

"I do trust you," I contended. "It's just that…"

"Good, then it's settled."

She turned abruptly and walked out of the room.

I hated when she did that. I fell backward onto the bed and looked up at the ceiling. I lay there for several minutes, feeling like I had just been trampled by a bull. I really needed this to be over soon. I don't care what anyone says, being married to a high-strung pregnant woman isn't for the faint of heart.

Carla seemed to enjoy the service. I wasn't overly worried about her being there with me, but it was important to me that she didn't overdo it. People were happy to see her, and several women rushed her right after the benediction. She was a bit of a hit with the congregation from the first day she attended. Everyone knew her from the news and treated her like she was a celebrity. Carla was used to that kind of attention and generally handled everything well. I stepped away so that she didn't feel like I was lurking behind her, but I never really took my eyes off of her— like a trained bodyguard.

There is no denying that her mood lifted immensely after seeing her friends at the church. She was a totally different person when we left for home. She talked nonstop in the car all the way home about nothing in particular without barely taking a breath. I just listened to her. Just as I pulled the car into the driveway, she shifted again.

"Um, I was thinking that maybe I could …"

"What?" I interrupted before I knew it. "What do you want to do now?"

"Whoa," she responded. "It's not that serious."

"Sorry," I said. "I didn't mean it."

"It's okay. I was just going to ask what you thought… about me going back to school to get a degree in counseling?"

"Counseling?" I questioned.

"Yeah, what do you think?"

"You don't want to go back to work at the news station?"

"I don't think I can with two kids, you know. I have a minor in psychology. I was thinking that I could be a clinical psychologist or something. Maybe I could have a home office and see people here."

"Is that something that you're really interested in doing?" I questioned. "You never said anything before."

"I think I might like it," she said. "Counseling has really helped me, you know, and I think that I can help other people."

"But I thought you said before that you want to travel the world witnessing history being made firsthand."

"Yeah, I did say that, but things have changed… I can't

imagine not being home with my kids.”

“Then I’m all for it if you are,” I related. “I just want you to be happy.”

“I am happy.”

I just looked at her.

“I know… I know … it doesn’t seem like it, but I haven’t exactly been myself lately,” she admitted. “My body has taken control and is doing its own thing. I hate being a burden to people.”

“You’re not a burden,” I insisted.

“Yes, I am. Like this, I am.”

“No, you’re not!” I insisted. “You’re being too hard on yourself.”

“I feel like my family has been worried about me ever since I was attacked… since high school,” she articulated. “Since then, it has been one thing after another with me. I thought I had finally made it, but here we go again. I just want to be normal and have a normal life.”

“I’m sorry, but that can never happen,” I asserted.

She froze.

“Why not?”

“Because you aren’t normal,” I claimed. “You’re like one in a million. You need to face it.”

“Thank you, baby,” she said with a smile.

We kissed and held each other tight.

I didn’t think anything could possibly feel better than love swirling inside. It’s clear that she had no idea what she did to me. I was addicted to her. My heart was wide-open.

We sat there alone together in our driveway for about an hour. For some reason, we both liked to sit in the parked car together and talk. There were moments when we didn’t say a word. We didn't have to; we could somehow look right into each other's heart. The world kept disappearing when we were alone.

The old me would have been convinced that something bad was about to happen at any moment and would have worried myself out of my mind. Even more, I would have internalized my fear and paranoia to the point of depression and self-loathing, but that was no longer the case as I was standing on my faith and actively resisting negative thoughts— something that really wasn't that hard for me to do after all, once I focused.

Honestly, Carla played a big part in my transformation. She wasn't a negative person at all. Her issue was that she carried a lot of guilt and shame from her past and needed to learn to forgive herself. I think that I helped her with that. In return, much of the way that she perceived the world spilled over onto me and affected my self-image positively. We were good for each other in almost every way.

This pregnancy wasn't planned. I somehow managed to keep my vow to the Lord and remained celibate the entire time that we were engaged – but just barely. Just as she predicted, that ended up being harder to do than I thought it would be. I missed being close to her like that, and it just got harder the closer we got to the wedding. After we were married, we were reckless a few times, and apparently, that's all it took.

But we were over the moon when we found out that we were going to have twins. Of course, I had twin sisters, but Carla didn't have any twins in her family. It was hard at first to get our heads around what was happening. It felt like a real blessing from God.

We had a lot of questions. The doctor explained that while 40 weeks is the full gestation period of the average pregnancy, most twins are delivered around 36 weeks. We talked about some of the common risks, such as premature babies and developmental delays, but he said that because Carla was healthy, he didn't expect any problems. She just needed to be closely monitored.

It was off-the-chain when we told our families. Her mother cried, and her father danced. My grandmother did a little jig. We were so happy. We were turning yet another corner— headed for forever. If this was a dream, I didn't want to wake up.

"I still can't believe that we are going to have a baby— twins, no less," she said.

"I know."

"Are you scared, Sam?"

"*Scared*? No, not exactly."

"Then what?" she asked and cuddled up to me in the bed. "Worried?"

"Grateful, I think."

"You're not worried a little?"

"I'm cautiously optimistic."

"Sounds like lawyer talk for *worried*.'"

"More like Christian talk for *prayerful*," I refuted. "I know that children are an inheritance from the Lord. So, I'm not scared. I'm excited to see what God is going to do, which could honestly be just about anything."

"I'm a little scared about all the things that could go wrong," she admitted.

"I heard what the doctor said, too, and it's probably normal to be a little scared." I articulated. "But fear is the enemy. I refuse to take the bait— been there and done that. God will bring us through. You'll see."

"What if He doesn't?" she posed. "Then what? Bad things happen to good people every day."

"I only know what I know." I contended.

"Well, I'm glad that you are so confident. It makes me feel calmer about everything."

"Good," I said.

"Do you want two boys or two girls or a mix— a boy and a girl?" she shifted.

"It doesn't really matter to me," I replied honestly. "What about you?"

"I think I want a mix," she expressed. "I can see now the two of them

running around the house screaming their heads off at the top of their lungs and breaking everything in sight."

"…Whoa, see now I'm scared," I declared. "That better not be my stuff they're tearing up!"

Chapter 6

Joe Carter called to say that they wanted to retain me to sue Longley Insurance Company and Robert Wells for wrongful termination and sexual harassment. The partners gave me the okay, so I was excited. Zoe came into the office herself to sign the retainer agreement, and we spoke only briefly. She said she was nervous, and I did what I could to reassure her. I told her that this would have been a big step for anybody.

"I know that it's a little scary, but for what it's worth, I think you're doing the right thing," I encouraged.

"Really?" she replied. "It feels crazy to me."

"Why *crazy*?"

"Because Bob is going to deny everything and he's a good liar," she replied. "Guys like him always win."

"No, they don't," I contested. "It just looks that way from the outside for a while."

"How can you be so sure?"

"That's a dangerous game to play because our lies have a way of turning on us," I preached. "They can't be trusted."

"He hates women, and he really hates me, especially now," she set forth. "I seriously doubt that he thinks that he's done anything wrong. That's why he'll never let me win."

"It's not about him," I maintained. "It's about you. Nobody gets to make you their victim because they don't respect some part of you, whether it's your sex or your race, or whatever. They just don't get to do that."

"I kinda feel like I was born with two strikes against me already," she articulated.

"What strikes?"

"Being Black and a woman."

"Maybe… so the main thing for you to do is to open up your stance, choke up on the bat, and make good contact," I advised.

"I don't think I understand."

"I'm sorry," I said. "I'm not really the one who should be using sports analogies. What I mean is sometimes all you need is one good pitch to knock the ball out of the park. Zoe, take your swing."

"Ah…Okay…"

"Let me tell you something," I shifted. "As soon as he starts lying, you should just start smiling inside because that means that you have already won. He knows that he's a punk … cause he's trying to cover up his own brokenness. But he picked the wrong girl this time and got exposed."

Her eyes lit up… for a second, before dimming again. But that was enough for me because I knew she heard me.

Honestly, this was a big deal for me, too. I had a lot to prove. I had never prepared a civil complaint before, and I wasn't sure that I had done it correctly. I agonized over every paragraph and rewrote it about fifty times. I wasn't even close to overcoming all of my own self-doubt.

I was in law school when law Professor Anita Hill

testified on Capitol Hill that her former boss, Clarence Thomas, had routinely sexually harassed her when she worked for him at the Department of Education. I wished that I had paid better attention because the arguments were a little tricky. The notion that a woman could sue their employers for harassment was still fairly new, stemming from the Civil Rights Act of 1964. While New York State had gradually implemented stricter policies, everything was still a bit unsettled.

The fact is that women were still hesitant to come forward with their complaints and face public scrutiny. I suddenly felt the weight of what we were trying to do. I literally prayed over the civil complaint before I filed it in the state supreme court and served the insurance company with the papers.

A week after I filed the complaint, I received a call from Scott Truman, a Utica lawyer, who represented the insurance company and Bob Wells. I felt my stomach do a backflip as I wasn't expecting him to call me. My first thought was that he was going to tell me that I had done something really stupid, and he was laughing at me.

"Sam, I don't believe that we have met before," he began.

"No, I don't think so."

"Well, we got your complaint in the Zoe Carter matter, and I was hoping that we could talk about this before I made the effort to draft our answer, and this thing goes any further."

"Sure, we can talk," I replied and swallowed hard.

"We were wondering if there was an easy way to make this go away."

"*Go away?*" I questioned. "What do you have in mind?"

"Perhaps a nominal settlement might be in order," he said. "We recognize that your client was let go without proper notice, and we might be willing to pay her two or three weeks' salary now for her trouble."

"I think we both know that that's not going to do it," I remarked. "My client has really suffered from this immensely. At this point, she doesn't have much to lose. She's already out of a job. But thanks for calling. I didn't really expect to hear from you at all, so I really appreciate it."

"What will do it?" he pressed.

"I don't really know, but we're not going to negotiate against ourselves."

"Then how about this?" Scott said. "I know that you are new to this. What do you say we fast-track this case and try to keep the costs down. Let me depose your client right away, and then after I hear her account of everything, then maybe I can come back to the table with another number that might be more to your liking."

"I would need to depose Mr. Wells first, seeing that his actions are what started everything."

"He denies that."

"Really?" I mocked. "I guess it's possible that we have the wrong guy."

"Well, you know how some of these young girls are," he answered with a slight chuckle. "They bite off a little more than they can chew."

"That's what he told his wife?" I wondered aloud. "Let me guess, he's irresistible to women."

"You know that the defendant has priority in

depositions not the plaintiff," he asserted. "We should go first."

"No, I didn't know that," I resisted.

"…Okay, so you're thinking just the one deposition for you then?" Scott shifted.

"And one for you," I replied. "Obviously, that could all change."

"Okay, I'll get our answer out to you within the next couple of days, and then I'll have my secretary call you to get some dates for the deposition," he remarked. "How does that sound?"

I know that it was just a phone call, but I enjoyed engaging with Scott Truman. I really missed the gamesmanship that is inherent between trial lawyers. He was clearly just trying to feel me out. I wasn't intimidated once we got to it. Frankly, I was eager to spar some more.

———•●•———

A new potential case was coming in almost every week now, mostly because the firm had a good reputation, and the partners knew a lot of people and effectively got the word out. I was learning how to screen through the inquiries for something that had legs. The ultimate question wasn't whether I thought the case was interesting, but rather whether the firm could make any real money from it.

One of my concerns before coming to the firm was that they would want me to work crazy hours, something like 50 and 60 hours a week, plus weekends. But, in actuality, nobody at McMann worked those kinds of hours. With Carla's condition, that would have been impossible for me to do. Typically, I was out the door by 8:00 a.m., and I got home around 6:00 p.m.

Carla's mom spent every other weekend at our house, and she was a big help. She came over on Friday nights and went home Sunday mornings. She was very worried about her daughter, which I understood. But I tried to gently suggest to her that maybe she might not want to crowd Carla too much. However, she wasn't really listening. So, there were a few sharp exchanges between the two of them, which I somehow managed to stay out of completely.

The mother/daughter dynamic was too much for me to even pretend to understand. Sometimes her sister Christina would come for a day with Jacob, her three-year-old son. Carla loved Jacob, but he was active and loud. I liked him too, but I was always glad when they left.

"Hi, Christina," I said as I walked into the kitchen.

"How was your meeting?" she asked.

"Good. How's Carla?"

"You mean the Queen of Sheba?"

"What?" I reacted.

"She's resting."

"Please don't call her that."

"I'm just kidding," she retreated. "I didn't mean anything."

"I know, but please don't call her that."

"Okay. I'm sorry."

"No problem."

"I made chicken cutlets for dinner," she said. "I hope that's all right."

"Great. Thank you."

Carla was lying on her back in bed, propped up by a

large pillow and watching the news. I knew that she missed it. I missed watching her on the air. She was a natural, and the camera loved her.

She was more than just another pretty face. There were a lot of attractive people on television, including those on the local news shows. But there was something about her that captured everyone's imagination. She was the only one who couldn't see it. I wasn't convinced that she could just walk away.

"Hey," I said and walked over and kissed her on the forehead."

"Hey, yourself."

"How are you feeling?"

"I'm good."

She was getting bigger in the middle every day. I loved it. She was also starting to look a little swollen, especially her hands and feet.

"Pastor said to tell you hello," I related.

"My mom is in her room with Jacob, and Christina is downstairs somewhere. You probably saw her."

"Yeah, she's making dinner. How's your head?"

"It doesn't hurt."

"Are you drinking your water?"

She pointed to the large glass pitcher on the nightstand.

"Can I get you something else?" I asked.

"No, I just want to watch the news."

"Then I'm gonna take a shower before dinner."

"Okay," she said and quickly redirected her attention back to the television.

Christina headed home to Rochester with Jacob right after dinner. I washed the dishes and cleaned the kitchen. Later, I fell asleep watching a movie alone in the living room while Carla and her mother watched something on the television in our room. She woke me up around 10:30 p.m., and I went up to bed and crashed.

"Sam!"

"What?"

"Sam!" Carla said again and shook me.

"Yeah," I whispered and opened my eyes.

"Sam, I got another nosebleed!"

I looked over, and her pillow was covered in blood. It looked like she had been shot in the head. I jumped out of bed and ran into the bathroom to get some towels. I tried to get her to put her head back, but she couldn't because too much blood was gushing out. My heart was racing.

"Get up!" I shouted. "We have to go to the ER!"

Exactly 15 minutes later, we were pulling into the parking lot at St. Luke's Hospital. Carla was in the backseat with her mother. Fortunately, it wasn't a busy night, and I was able to pull into a parking spot close to the door. I jumped out of the car, and scooped up Carla in my arms, and carried her inside.

"What's going on?" the attendant at the front desk asked.

"A bad nosebleed," I said. "She's pregnant."

"How far?"

"Thirty weeks."

"Who's your doctor?"

I drew a blank.

"O'Connor," Carla answered.

"Can you walk, honey?" the nurse inquired.

Carla nodded.

"Can you put her down, please?" the woman urged.

"No, I will not!" I exclaimed. "She needs to see a doctor now!"

My terse response startled everyone, even me, because I didn't just say it, I owned it too. It came from a place deep inside that I had long forgotten was there.

"Sir, I just need to see her stand to do an assessment."

"Sam, it's okay," Carla said and lowered her feet to the ground. She was holding a bloody towel up to her nose with both hands."

"Does anything else hurt?"

"I have a headache, and my side hurts a little."

"Where does your side hurt?"

"Over here," Carla responded and pointed to her upper right side near the rib cage.

"Is it sharp or more like a throbbing pain?"

"Burning."

"Do you feel any cramps or pressure like you're in labor?"

"Labor?" Carla reacted. "No, nothing like that."

Just then, a man in dark blue hospital scrubs rushed over with a wheelchair and indicated to Carla to sit down.

"You guys can follow me," he said.

Once we got into one of the side rooms, two male nurses rushed in. They put Carla on the bed, and one of them immediately started taking her blood pressure, and the other one was looking at her nose. Carla's mom and I stood back at a distance without saying a word.

"Her blood pressure is really high… I'm getting 178/118. We need the doctor stat."

Two more people came into the room. I assumed that the middled-aged white man in a white coat was the doctor. Now, the four of them surrounded Carla, and we couldn't see what they were doing. About a minute later, another nurse walked up to us and told us that we had to go to the waiting room and ushered us away.

We sat there nervously for about an hour. Finally, the same doctor approached.

"Mr. Hicks?" he asked.

"Yes."

"Hi, I'm Dr. Martin."

"Hi."

"We are going to admit your wife. I just spoke to Dr. O'Connor. and we need to run some blood work. You know she has toxemia, right?"

"*Toxemia*?"

"He may have called it *preeclampsia*. It's a serious complication of pregnancy. We see it sometimes with women who are carrying more than one baby. Her blood pressure is dangerously high, and there is significant protein in her urine."

"You said it's serious," Mrs. Jenkins interjected. "How serious?"

"It's pretty serious, I'd say, for both the mother and the babies," he responded. "We need to get her blood pressure down and look for signs of organ damage, like in the kidneys or liver. She will definitely not be carrying these babies full term, but it's too early to induce her at 30 weeks."

"When can she be induced?" I questioned.

"Typically, delivery is recommended around 37 weeks."

"Are you kidding me?" I exclaimed. "She can't do seven more weeks!"

"I know," he admitted. "But the babies need more time for lung development, which happens last in the fetus. That's their best chance for survival."

"So how much longer will you let her stay like this?" I pressed.

"That will be Dr. O'Connor's call. You're going to have to talk to him."

"He just told us that she was 'high risk' because she was carrying multiples, and her blood pressure was a big concern," I vented. "He didn't say anything about any *toxemia* or *preeclampsia*."

"Well, he took her out of work so that's clearly what he was thinking," Dr. Martin contended. "He's been following the protocol. I checked, and she has been seeing him pretty regularly."

"Are the babies okay now?" Carla's mom asked.

"There's no sign of fetal distress," he answered. "They have good, strong heartbeats."

"That's a relief," she uttered.

"She's in good hands," he reassured. "Dr. O'Connor is an outstanding obstetrician. We are going to take good care of her and believe the best."

This was all very unnerving, and I wasn't quite sure what to believe. I was thinking all along that if Carla just took it easy, she would deliver normally. I went with her to all of her most recent doctor appointments, and I listened very carefully to everything they said. While they were thorough in the examinations, they never sounded any alarms either. They had been mostly supportive and upbeat.

I get that they probably didn't want to scare us and that there are no guarantees in the practice of medicine, but I also felt a little like we had been tricked, so I was angry too. We had a right to know everything. On her last visit, Dr. O'Connor said everything looked good. I definitely wasn't expecting all of this, as I was believing God for something very different for us.

Chapter 7

My grandmother loved going to church with us, and she went a lot. She befriended two white ladies, who were about her age, and they liked to sit together front and center and stand there together after service, socializing. Carla told me that they each had a crush on Gus, one of our deacons, and they loved to talk and speculate about him. I felt sorry for poor Gus, who I'm pretty sure had no idea what his smile did to them.

Mama's life had changed for the better in the last year after my mother died. She came out of her shell a little and was interacting with more people outside of the neighborhood. She started taking the bus alone and could get to my house by herself. She seemed to really enjoy her newfound independence. I was proud of her.

But Carla's health was a pressing concern for Mama, too, which she was struggling to manage as well. Somewhere along the way, she had come to really care about Carla. I don't know if my mother's death had anything to do with it, but for some reason, she was much more sentimental and emotional than she used to be. Although I didn't see it myself, I was told that she cried at my wedding. It was a vast improvement overall as she seemed to be a happier person.

However, she freely expressed her inner fears about Carla and the babies, which wasn't necessarily something that I wanted to hear. Wise men think before speaking.

"Y'all just got married and starting out in life together, and I feel so bad," she expressed in the car on the drive home from church one Sunday. "What's happening to you guys is really not fair."

"It's just a part of life," I replied. "Nobody knows why these things happen. Thinking like that leads to a dead-end because there are just too many things that we aren't supposed to know or understand yet."

"You really believe that?" she resisted. "Cause to my way of thinking, too much bad stuff happens to the good people."

"Who are these good people?" I wondered.

"You and Carla both are good," she insisted. "Nobody can ever tell me any different. Johnnie Mae's daughter, that wild one who wears all that makeup and is always walking around with her tail out, she got all of them kids with all these different men. She keeps popping them out like biscuits, and she don't know how to take care of even one of them, not a one! You ask me, she's the one who should be sick with high blood pressure!"

"Mama, that's a terrible thing to say," I rebuked. "You know better than that."

"Maybe, but I'm speaking the truth, and you know I am," she dug in. "That girl is around here running around with every rascal she meets, and poor Carla's got to suffer like she has been."

"But we don't think like that," I urged. "It's unloving

and…ugly."

"I don't know why you wouldn't," she pressed. "You ain't never done anything to hurt nobody. I think you deserve to have all the children you want."

"Thanks, but only Jesus is truly good because He is the only one who is without sin. He doesn't owe us anything."

"Did they say if this here disease happens more to Black women than white?" she asked.

"Why does that matter?"

"Boy, just tell me," she insisted. "Sometimes I don't know about you. There is such a thing as too much schooling."

"Um, yes to your question," I spoke. "I think that it's a little more common in Black women, but it really doesn't happen that much overall. Nobody knows why it happens to some women."

"That's what I'm talkin' about," Mama said. "Black folks just have it harder. It's true. It seems like you guys have already been through enough."

"I know, but we're really blessed too," I explained. "We have each other and a great life. We can get through this."

"Sure, you're right," she said. "I'm just say'n y'all keep running into trouble head on."

"Mama, you have to try to stay positive," I asserted.

"Your mother didn't have no problems when she was carrying Tasha and Tonya," she digressed. "But she was just a young girl too, and I think that the young girls carry better on account that their bodies are naturally stronger."

"I don't know," I said.

"I hear tell that some of these babies who they have to take early out of the womb have all kinds of problems in life," Mama mentioned. "Did this here doctor say anything about that?"

"We're trying not to focus on any of that stuff," I explained. "The important thing now is to make it to the point where the babies can be safely delivered."

"Oh, I know that's right," she replied. "I'm just thinking out loud to myself. You know how I go on sometimes."

"…Yeah, I know."

Obviously, the edges of Mama's thinking were still in the process of being softened… as were my own. But she really did have a good heart, no matter how it sometimes looked or sounded. Not that it's an excuse, but it's easy to lose proper perspective when the devil beats you up enough and steals your joy. Scripture tells us that God blesses those who are poor in heart and realize their need for Him.

"Are you sure you don't want me to go up to the hospital more and give you a break?" she solicited. "I ain't doing nothin but sitting at home worrying myself sick anyway. I could keep her company while you're at work."

"Um…her mom is here, and the rest of her family is in and out all the time. Carla isn't always good with that. There's such a thing as too much company."

"Okay, but just let me know what y'all need me to do, you hear?"

"Okay, we will."

"I just feel kinda helpless, broken up, you know," she expressed. "That's all."

"Yeah, I know," I acknowledged andand our eyes locked for a second.

We were both silent for a while after that. I was thinking about my mother for some reason. Thoughts of her frequently came to me out of nowhere. I had learned that the best thing to do when that happened was to let them run their course like the flu and not to fight against them.

But I was also reminiscing about a time not that long ago when my drug of choice was feeling sorry for myself, and I was slowly dying alone on the long, darkened road to nowhere. Coming out of the darkness was the best thing that ever happened to me, better than Carla even. So, there was no way that I was ever going back there again, no matter what. That was my quiet resolve.

"…Maybe you should call Deacon Gus to come over to console you?" I finally said. "I know you want to."

She turned her head and shoulders sharply toward me and looked me up and down.

"What did you say?" she demanded.

"You heard me," I mocked and looked back at her, this time with disapproving eyes.

She suddenly began cackling and coughing at the same time. I thought she was going to choke.

"I heard it's getting kind of hot and heavy with you and him," I teased. "You should be ashamed of yourself— in God's house no less."

"Who told you that?" she asked, and struggled to hide her stubborn grin. "You know that ain't me— that's Katherine and Sadie."

"That's not what I heard," I continued. "Mama, you know you're too old to be playing kissy face."

"Who you calling *old*?" she challenged.

"If the shoe fits…"

"Hmm, don't make me knock you over the head with this here shoe," she threatened.

"Why are you getting so nervous, huh?" I poked again. "I just don't want you to let that white man break your heart."

"Child, please, I ain't studying that man," she claimed. "I keep trying to tell you that."

"You just don't want me to know," I asserted.

"Hmm, did Carla tell you that?"

"Doesn't matter who told me," I deflected. "You should have been the one to tell me instead of keeping your little *love* secrets."

"Boy, you're so crazy!" she expressed. "You better leave me out of that mess if you know what's good for you!"

* ● *

Dr. O'Connor said that Carla was going to be in the hospital for the rest of her pregnancy. Her liver enzymes were elevated, too. They had her on a lot of different medications, including something to reduce the risk of seizures. She was tired and slowing down, both physically and mentally.

Her mother had basically moved into our house. She only went back home when it was absolutely necessary for her to do so. Carla's dad was at our house a lot, too. We took shifts being at the hospital so that Carla was rarely alone during the day.

The partners at the firm were very understanding of my situation, but since we billed our clients by the hour, I was determined to put my time in. I started going into the office at 6:00 a.m. I went to the hospital around noon every day for an hour and didn't eat lunch. I went back to work for five hours before going home for a quick bite to eat and then I rushed back out to sit with Carla until midnight.

"You know, you don't have to be here all the time," Carla voiced.

"I'm not here all the time."

"You are overdoing it," she asserted.

"I'm good."

"Why don't you just work a normal day and then come here after work?"

"That's pretty much what I'm doing."

"No, it's not," she refuted. "You're here during the day, too."

"I got this," I said.

"If you kill yourself, I'll never forgive you!" she expressed.

"You're overreacting a little, don't you think?" I defended.

"When the babies are born, there's going to be more stress and things to do with the feedings and everything," she pointed out. "That's in like a month. You're not going to make it if you burn yourself out completely before we even get there."

"You don't have to worry about me," I maintained.

"But I do worry about you," she asserted. "I worry about you all the time. I'd feel a lot better if I knew that you were taking care of yourself. We need some normalcy in the middle of all this crazy business."

"I hate the thought of you being up here alone," I persisted.

"I'm not alone. Your grandmother is here a lot. And people from the station and church, too. Actually, it's too much for me sometimes."

"I know, but…"

"You know I need my alone time," she argued. "I had to tell my mother the same thing. I want her to go back to her life as much as possible and start going back home to my dad during the week."

I didn't say anything, but I didn't like that she did that without telling me first. I liked that her mother was there when I couldn't be. She was the only one whom I really trusted. I tried to hide my despair.

"Sam?"

I just looked at her. She looked determined.

"You know I'm right," she contended. "You are still new at your job, and I know that's stressful for you too."

"I don't …"

"How about this?" she presented. "We just try it. You can come here every day after work. But not in the middle of the day anymore."

"…Okay, but…"

"And you eat and sleep right."

"I'm getting enough sleep," I claimed.

"And you have to go to church on Sunday. You love it there and it's good for you because it recharges your batteries."

"I only missed a couple of Sundays," I contested.

"C'mon, Sam. You're not listening. Can you please try? For me?"

I sighed heavily.

"I don't know what you want me to say," I resisted.

"I'm not rejecting you or anything, you know," she implored. "I just really need you to be at your best because …I can't do this without you. There's just no way!"

Tears suddenly flowed freely from her eyes like a waterfall. I stepped closer to her bedside and rubbed her right shoulder.

"All right, all right," I caved. "We'll do it your way. It'll all work out. You'll see."

I kissed the side of her face and held her in my arms. She cried hard for a couple of minutes. I hated seeing her like this. It made me feel helpless— again.

Chapter 8

At first, I thought Zoe had dropped the phone after I told her that her deposition was scheduled for the following week. We were going to take Bob Wells' testimony first at his attorney's office and her deposition was going to be the following day at my office.

"Are you there?" I asked.

"Um, yeah, I'm here…sorry."

"I already told you that you can do this," I said.

"I know, but I don't think you understand."

"Then explain it to me," I insisted.

"I can't," she contended. "Is Bob going to be there for my testimony?"

"Probably, but I will be sitting right next to you. There might be a representative from the insurance company there, too. There won't be anyone else there except for the stenographer."

"Can my mom come?"

"Not if they don't want her there?"

"I don't understand why they would care," she complained.

"They're going to say that she's influencing your

testimony."

"Just by watching?"

"Yes."

"Can I be there when he testifies?"

"Yes."

"Um… you said before that they… can ask me anything about my personal life?"

"Yes, basically."

"And I have to answer those kinds of questions?"

"It depends. They can ask you anything relevant to the lawsuit."

"Why would *my* personal life be *relevant* to whether Bob kept trying to put his hands on me?"

"Because we are claiming that his actions affected you *personally,* and have impacted your life in a very real and significant way," I explained.

"I see…"

"Is there something that you want to tell me before you testify?" I asked.

"Something like what?"

"I don't know," I replied. "But it sounds like you might be worried about being asked about something in particular."

"… Uh, no, not really… I just don't like the idea of it. Seems like an invasion of my privacy."

"That's because it *is* an invasion of your privacy," I emphasized. "And it's important that you see it for what it is. When you sue somebody, you are putting it all out there."

"I just never knew that before," she claimed.

"Most people have no idea how the legal system really works until they experience it for themselves."

"I just never thought it would be so… *icky.*"

"Life is hard, and most of us have to fight for something," I asserted. "And unfortunately, women in particular have to fight in this world… especially Black women."

"How would you know that?" she boldly asked.

"Um…because I deeply love a Black woman who has struggled from time to time."

"Oh," she reacted. "I'm sorry… I probably shouldn't have asked you that. I'm really…"

"No, it's okay," I replied. "I don't mind. You see, I'm just discovering that there's a private side and a public side to everything that happens to us."

"What do you mean?"

"Do you believe in God, Zoe?"

"Yes, I do. We're catholic."

"God rarely gives us anything… any gift …or lesson, or treasure for us to keep to ourselves," I explained. "We are supposed to love and bless other people. Even our pain is supposed to be shared, too, because one person's pain can be the very thing that brings another person through the same or similar thing. That's why I think that it's a mistake to completely hide ourselves from the world."

"I never thought of it like that before," she replied.

"I never really saw it either," I admitted.

"This woman you love is very lucky."

"I'm not sure I believe in luck."

"Why is that?"

"Because some things are just meant to be."

She was silent on the other end of the phone. I never meant for our conversation to get philosophical or religious. It felt less than professional somehow. But she pulled it out of me, so I wasn't sorry for telling her those things.

"I need you to come in sometime this week to be prepped," I regrouped. "It'll only take about an hour. Can you come in on Friday afternoon?"

"Yes, I think so. My new job with the county doesn't start for another week."

"How about 3 o'clock?" I asked.

"Okay. Thanks."

My gut told me that she was hiding something. I had no idea what it could be, but I could tell that it was oppressing her and inhibiting her thoughts and dreams. She reeked of sadness, the way I used to be.

I never doubted for a second that Bob Wells did exactly what she said he did, and maybe more. But people are complicated, so it's hard to know for sure what anyone is really thinking at any given point in time. The important takeaway here for me was that my client didn't fully trust me, which was obviously something that I had dealt with many times before."

However, I knew enough not to take anything that a client might say or do too personally. While I had still only been an attorney for almost six years, it was definitely a long six years. I had considerable experience compared to most young lawyers my age, and I had learned the hard way not to get too personally invested in any one case. In the end, the client calls the shots, meaning Zoe could change her mind at any moment and decide that she wanted to discontinue her lawsuit, leaving me locked and loaded without a target.

But the undeniable truth was that I liked her. Being mixed-race was probably not always the easiest thing to be. I really didn't know much about it. I never had a close friend before who was biracial, nor had I ever spoken personally to someone who knew about it firsthand. Obviously, she was the whole package physically. But outer beauty, like everything else, can be both a curse and a blessing, depending on how it is internalized.

Zoe arrived on time, with her father, for our appointment to go over her testimony. I explained to her the basic ground rules of deposition. They really aren't that complicated, but anything a witness says at a deposition can be used against them later at trial. The most important thing was to listen closely to the question before answering and to never guess, which was much harder to do than it might otherwise seem.

She said that she understood everything when I finished talking, and that she didn't have any questions. But I wasn't convinced that she really did.

"What if this lawyer tries to put words in her mouth?" Joe Carter asked.

"That's why I'm there to see that that doesn't happen," I explained.

"Tell me why my wife and I can't be there," he pressed. "Zoe told me that you said we can't come. I don't get why we can't just sit in the back of the room. We won't say anything."

"This is not the trial, it's a deposition under oath," I explained. "They may decide at some point down the road that they want to depose either one of you, too, and they don't want you to have heard Zoe's testimony."

"Why would they want to question us?"

"I don't know, they probably won't," I replied. "But one of the purposes of the deposition is to find any information that might be relevant to your case. It's hard to know what is going to be relevant to your case a year from now."

He shook his head back and forth in disbelief.

"But I think the main reason is that they don't want you to be able to support her through it," I said. "They want her in *the hot seat* all by herself."

"And I don't think that's very fair," Mr. Carter complained and looked dejected. "That's making her a victim all over again!"

He threw his hands up in the air, leaned back in his chair, and silently fumed.

"You can be at the trial… I mean, if this ends up going to trial," I offered.

He didn't say anything, but I could tell that my answer still wasn't acceptable to him.

"I'm sorry, but it's really not that big of a deal," I said. "Zoe is smart, and she's telling the truth about what happened. She'll do great!"

"…Okay," he muttered and looked away.

I meant what I said about Zoe, which was as much for her benefit as to appease her seemingly protective father. It was important that she knew that I believed in her. I had no idea how aggressive or mean-spirited Scott Truman was going to be. She needed to be able to fight back and not fall to pieces when she is asked a question she doesn't like.

Honestly, I was actually more concerned about myself than I was about Zoe. I had never deposed anyone before, and I still had to prepare my own questions for Bob Wells. Everyone said that depositions are easy to do because they are so informal and there is no judge or jury present. Regardless, although I liked challenges generally, it was always hard for me to be confident when trying something new, especially in public.

I watched the interaction between Zoe and her father closely, and I thought I noticed some tension or separation between the two of them. Although he said the right things, they never looked directly at each other. Her body was shifted away from him much of the time, and she shielded herself from him with her hair. It felt a little like I was having two separate conversations with them.

Obviously, I had no idea if there really was anything negative going on between them. Good trial attorneys must be able to read body language and be willing to trust their intuition about what they are seeing and sensing. Words alone never give the full picture because some important communications are never spoken. My parting thought was that it might be for the best after all if Joe Carter wasn't there looking over her shoulder while she gave her testimony.

• ● •

A woman named Susan Wright made an appointment to see me. She just called the office and said that she was looking for a lawyer to handle her medical malpractice case against an area hospital. She asked for me by name. I never spoke to her, and Kim, our receptionist, scheduled her to come in for a consultation.

She was taken to our conference room when she arrived. Our office policy was that new or potential clients were not to be left sitting in the waiting room. I jumped up from my desk as soon as Kim told me that my appointment had arrived.

"Hi, I'm Sam Hicks."

Hi, I'm Susan Wright," she replied and extended her right hand.

She was a middle-aged white woman, with shoulder-length brown hair, a small pointy nose, and round glasses. She was seated at the conference room table when I walked in, so I couldn't see all of her, but she appeared to be of average height and weight. She was wearing a white top, brown slacks, and flat shoes."

"Mrs. Wright, what brings you here today?" I asked.

"Oh, please no," she said and waved me off with her left hand. "Please call me Sue."

"Sue," I obliged.

"Well, my husband Mike died last year."

"I'm very sorry to hear."

"Thank you," she said softly.

"How can we help you?" I inquired.

"My niece, Lori Bennet, works over at the courthouse, and she said that she knew you and that you are a very good lawyer."

"Yes, I know Lori. She works in the probation department."

"Yes, that's her."

"That was very kind of her to say. Please give her my best."

"I will."

"So, tell me what happened to your husband," I encouraged.

"He had a massive stroke and died," she whispered. "He was just 52 years old."

"Oh my!" I exclaimed.

"He was complaining about having a bad headache for a couple of days that wouldn't go away. He also said he felt weak and a heaviness all over and that the light was hurting his eyes. I finally took him to the ER."

"What Hospital?"

"St. Luke's."

"St. Luke's, really?" I reacted.

"They ran several tests and did an MRI and a CT scan. They thought it might be meningitis or an infection. He was in the hospital for two days. Then they sent him home with some new anti-seizure medication. But his headaches didn't go away, and he started vomiting. My daughter, Abbey, and I decided that we needed to take him to a hospital in Syracuse, and he had a stroke in the car before we got there. He died the next day."

"How long was he home before you decided to take him to Syracuse?"

"A week."

"Would you say his symptoms got worse during that week before he started the vomiting?"

"Yes, they did."

"Did you tell his doctors that he was getting worse?"

"Mike didn't want to go back to the hospital," she advised. "He was a pretty strong guy, a mechanic who liked hard work. He was a healthy guy his whole life and this was the first time that he was ever really sick like that. I could see if he had a bad heart or was out of shape and smoked, or something. But he was none of those things."

"What do you think the doctors at St. Luke's did wrong?"

"I don't really know," she admitted. "I'm not a doctor,

but I think they discharged him too early, that's for sure. No one told us that he was at risk of having a stroke. I'm telling you that it all doesn't add up. Everything happened so fast, and now I don't have a husband … and my children and grandchildren have lost their father and grandpa."

She began to cry a little, and I sat completely still while she struggled to regain her composure. My thought was that she was probably every bit as strong as her husband was.

"Well, I'm not a doctor either," I finally spoke. "You're going to have to get a copy of his medical records and have them reviewed by a doctor. You can't bring a lawsuit for medical malpractice without a doctor's signed affirmation saying that the doctors' at St. Luke's did something wrong."

"How do I get that?" she asked with a frustrated look on her face.

"A lawyer can help you do that," I replied. "If we represented you, we would try to find someone. There are a lot of doctors out there who do this kind of thing all the time. I don't think they are too hard to find."

"Will you represent me?"

"I have to present your case to the partners here, and they will decide whether we take this. Is that something you want me to do?"

"Yes, please."

"Is there anything else that you want me to know before I do that?"

"Ah…I can't really think of anything. But I guess I do want you to know that this is about more than the money to me."

"I never thought that."

"You see, Mike and I were born on the same day," she

said. "Can you believe that? I mean, what are the odds? But I don't think that it was just a coincidence. We met after high school, and we were married for 33 years."

"Really? That long?"

"I tell you this man was as much a part of me as my own body," she asserted. "And I loved him so much that sometimes it scared me. The only thing that I loved more than him was the way that he loved me, which, let me tell you, was sweeter than pure honey! I lost everything when he died …"

This time, she lowered her head, and the dam to her heart and soul finally burst. She clutched her chest and leaned forward in great emotional pain. I quickly jumped to my feet, got the box of tissues off the top of the bookshelf in the corner, and put it directly in front of her. Without lifting her head, she took one and covered her face with it.

I felt her pain completely in that moment, but I chose to hide it and show no reaction.

"I'm so sorry… I …I…didn't mean to do this," she blubbered. "I'm still not myself."

"It's okay," I whispered. "I think I get it."

"I wonder if it's possible to love another person too much?" she questioned and looked up at me intently in a way that made me uncomfortable.

Her chest rose and fell with rapid breaths. The question came out of left field, but it really resonated with me and distracted me for a moment.

"Um, I don't know," I replied.

"Me either," she contended. "But what else can you do after you've been kissed by an angel?"

Chapter 9

When I walked into Carla's private room, she and Mama were watching television. My first thought was that I hoped that Mama hadn't been there all day and overstayed her welcome.

"Hi, Sam!" Carla said.

"Hey, yourself," she responded and smiled brightly. "How are you doing?"

"I'm good."

"I missed you," I said and leaned in and kissed her slow.

"I missed you, too."

"Hi, Mama."

"Hi, Sam."

"How long have you been here?"

"Not long," Mama replied. "I came up right after my soap opera went off. I was just waiting for you to get here."

"Do you want a ride home?"

"No, no. I can take the bus."

"You sure?"

"Yeah, I'm sure. It don't make no sense for you to have to drive me home and then turn around and come all the way back."

Mama stood up and started gathering her things.

"You don't have to rush off on my account," I said with a smirk. "Unless you are expecting a gentleman caller."

"Sam, I thought I already told you about playing with me," she admonished and cut her eyes at me.

"Thank you for coming," Carla said. "I enjoyed our talk."

"Me too," Mama remarked. "You remember what I said. You have to stay positive. This too shall pass."

I smiled to myself.

"Y'all both try to get some sleep, hear," she directed. "Them babies gonna be here before you know it."

"Okay, thanks, Mama."

"Oh, you're welcome," she replied.

She waved and walked out of the room.

"So, how are you really doing?"

"No, I'm feeling okay," Carla replied. "I wish I could find a comfortable position in this bed. It's hard to sleep."

"Did you see Dr. O'Connor today?"

"Yes, he was here earlier, before your grandmother got here."

"Any update on when he is planning to induce you?"

"No."

"What did he say?"

"He just said that my blood pressure is good. Just slightly elevated, and the swelling in my legs is actually going down a little. Look, see."

She pulled back the blanket so that I could see both of her legs.

"They do look better," I agreed. "Except for maybe that one big toe there that looks kinda like a miniature donut."

"No, it doesn't!" she exclaimed.

"Yes, it does," I insisted. "Especially if you squint your eyes a little when you look at it. Go ahead and try."

"That's not funny," she reacted. "And now I'm mad at you!"

She kind of crinkled up her nose and pouted like she tended to do sometimes. I loved to see her do that.

"C'mon, you know I'm just playing," I said.

"No, you're right," she reconsidered. "My feet look terrible!"

"No, they don't."

"Yes, they do!" she maintained. "I can't take care of myself. My hair is a mess. I can't even see my feet most of the time."

"Give yourself a break," I pleaded. "You are about to give birth to twins, not trying to win a beauty pageant. There are two miracles in you."

"That's kinda what your grandmother was just saying—about how women are the crown of God's creation. She said that we were *designed* special, not just created like men."

"She's right."

"I know she is," Carla reacted.

"Besides, you still look sexy to me!" I declared.

"*Sexy?*" she scoffed. "Something is wrong with you."

"I'm just missing my snuggle bunny."

"Is that right?"

"Uh-huh, I wish there was a way for me to prove it to you."

"That's how I got here, you proving it to me," she said. "This is all your fault, you know."

"I don't recall you complaining at the time."

"Well, I was distracted," she said and laughed. "I'm never letting you touch me again."

"We'll see about that," I resisted. "You know I have ways of making you change your mind."

"Good luck with that," she rebuked

"I want you to know that your words are painful," I joked.

"I think you'll live," she said.

"What's that?" I wondered and nodded toward a book or something that was sticking out from underneath her pillow.

"Um…it's a book of baby names."

"What?"

"It has all of the most popular baby names to choose from."

"I never knew that there was a book like that out there," I admitted.

"My sister gave it to me."

"Did you find anything you like?"

I plopped myself down on the bed next to her, and she moved over to make room for me.

"There are quite a few good ones," she indicated.

She opened the book.

"Like what?"

She started flipping through the pages.

"See here, I like the name *Maya* for a girl. What do you think?"

"It's all right, but what other names go with it?" I asked.

"See, that's the problem. I'm having trouble coming up with two matching names that I like."

"Do they have to match?" I questioned. "We don't even

know the sex of the babies."

"I know, but I think it's cute when they match. Don't you? It's like a special connection."

"They're twins," I replied. "That's already a special connection."

"Right, but this makes it that much more special."

"What about *Ike* and *Mike* if they are boys?" I asked.

"I'm not naming my baby Ike. You must be out of your mind!"

"What about *Floyd* and *Lloyd*?" I railed. "Or maybe *Ricky* and *Lucy*?"

She rolled her eyes.

"Are you even trying?" she challenged.

"I'm doing the best I can," I purported.

"No, you're not!"

"You pick," I insisted. "I just want veto power."

"Sam, I want to do this together," she whined.

"This is us doing it together."

"No, it's not," she refuted.

"You are just going to shoot down all of my suggestions anyway," I maintained. "So, you come up with a list of names out of this book that you like, and then we'll go from there. Besides, you're the one doing all of the hard work. You should have first say."

"All right, but you are no fun, I tell you."

"*Fun* is overrated in my book," I expressed. "At this point, we just gotta get 'er done!

"I don't know— maybe."

"Oh, by the way, the mailman left a big box by the garage door for you," I reported. "Did you order something?"

"No, not that I recall. You should have opened it."

"It has your name on it," I said.

"I don't care."

"I wasn't sure, so I just stuck it in the corner."

"Somebody probably sent a gift for the babies," she surmised.

"Yeah, that's probably it."

Chapter 10

Unfortunately, the partners at the firm decided against taking Susan Wright's case. They wanted to refer the case to an attorney they had worked with several times in the past, who handled strictly medical malpractice cases. Apparently, they got a referral fee from that attorney, which could be fairly hefty depending upon how much money the attorney actually recovered.

"I know that you are disappointed Sam, but we feel that at this point in your transition to civil practice, it makes sense to refer the case to a more experienced attorney," Tony explained.

"I'm willing to do the work," I replied. "I really think I can learn it pretty fast."

"We know that you are smart," Tony complimented. "But there is no one here who can help you with this, and frankly, this case is far from a slam dunk. Even if you found an expert neurologist, or whoever, to support your case, there is still a decent chance that the jury will find that the hospital didn't do anything wrong. You said it yourself, the husband delayed going back to the hospital when his symptoms worsened. It sounds complicated, and it's going to cost us a lot of money to get this case prepared for trial."

"…Okay, I think I understand," I made myself say.

"I'll call the Wright woman myself and explain everything to her and hopefully get her connected up with Anthony Romani."

"Thanks."

He hesitated.

"Look, Sam, if you're really interested in medical malpractice as a practice area for this firm, then get yourself trained in that area of the law," he advised. "There are seminars and conferences everywhere that you can go to and learn more about it. We are not saying no forever, just no for now."

"All right, I appreciate you considering it," I obliged.

"No problem."

"I admire your heart," he said. "I really do. I hope you never lose that."

I didn't quite know what to say.

"How's your wife doing?" he asked.

"She's hanging in there. It's been a long road for us, you know."

"I can only imagine," Tony sympathized. "I was stressed out and completely out of my mind both times when my wife was pregnant, and she just had normal births with no complications. You guys are real troopers."

"What we are is tired," I said.

"Oh, I'm sure," he replied. "But I want you to know that we want to be as supportive of you both as we can be. So, please don't hesitate to let us know what you need. I have no idea how you are holding it together the way that you are."

"In two weeks, the babies should be here, and then we

can go from there," I articulated.

"I hate to break it to you, pal, but that's when the real games begin. Take it from me. I know firsthand."

---·●·---

"How's Lacey?" I wondered.

"Who?"

I just looked at him.

"Oh… oh, Lacey," Pastor said. "I didn't hear you clearly."

"Are you still counseling her?"

"Why do you ask?"

"How come you don't want to answer me?" I posed and took a big sip of my coffee.

I gestured to the waitress that I wanted more coffee.

"It's not that," he replied. "Counseling is supposed to be confidential."

"Oh, give me a break!" I scoffed. "You already know that I know that you've been meeting with her about her marriage."

"I just think that I need to be careful about what I say to anyone about her."

"Why?"

"Because it's the right thing to do," he contended.

"So, what I'm hearing is that you are still meeting with her," I asserted.

"I didn't say that."

You didn't have to."

"Look, I already told you that nothing improper is happening here," Pastor emphasized.

"I don't think that her husband believes that."

"I don't care what he believes."

"You'd better care," I reiterated. "I don't understand why you can't just walk away. Is it possible that you are more emotionally invested in her than you care to admit?"

"No, I don't think that's the case."

"Then what gives?" I wondered. "Why aren't you willing to let someone else counsel her?"

"Because she won't accept anyone else," he presented.

"How do you know?"

"Because she told me."

"What did she tell you exactly?"

"She said that she will only talk to me. She begged me."

"Is she blackmailing you?"

"Not exactly."

"What then?"

"I may have let her kiss me."

"*Let her kiss you*?" I repeated allowed. "What are you even saying?"

I didn't initiate it."

"How did you respond?"

"I pushed her away," he explained.

"Eventually," I asserted.

"Yes, something like that," he whispered and quickly looked away. "That's all it was, though— I swear."

"How long ago did this happen?"

"A while back."

"But still you kept meeting with her?"

His eyes got big, and he slowly put his head down.

"And now she's pressuring you because she wants more from you," I concluded. "Is that it?"

"In a nutshell."

"Why didn't you tell me this before?"

"Because I was embarrassed and ashamed."

"Are you in love with Lacey?"

"No, I certainly am not in love with her!"

"You sure?"

"I love my wife. This was nothing to me, just a momentary lapse in judgment. I didn't know what to do. I didn't want to …offend her."

"Is she in love with you?"

"She says she is," he disclosed.

"So, her husband does have reason to be jealous of you?" I stressed.

"Not really…Maybe… I don't know."

"How do you see this ending?" I questioned.

"I just want Lacey to be safe and happy."

"Wrong answer!" I argued.

"What do you mean?"

"I think most guys in your situation, especially now, would just want her to go on with her life and leave them out of it— there's just too much at stake."

"Maybe, but I'm not like most guys."

"Maybe that's why you're in this predicament," I countered.

"What's that supposed to mean?"

"I think you know," I charged. "She got to you, we both know it. And now you're emotionally invested in another woman."

"Wait a minute," Pastor demanded. "I don't think that I have done anything wrong. She kissed me. I'm not interested in her romantically."

"The devil is wise in his deceptions," I insisted. "He sets traps for us."

"That sounds a little callous to me if you don't mind me saying," he replied. "Her life is in complete shambles."

"My guess is that pastors get tested more than we regular believers, not less," I ventured to say. "Am I right? Are you telling me they didn't teach you that in Bible college?"

"You know, sometimes you are pretty hard to take," he asserted.

"I don't know what to tell you. I'm just a lawyer, not a pastor."

"Then, what do you think I should do now that you know everything?" Pastor asked.

"Tell her it's over and walk away clean!"

"I see," he remarked.

"I don't like her," I said pointedly.

"You don't know her."

"Neither do you!" I fired back and laughed. "What I *do know* is that she shouldn't be kissing someone else's husband, no matter how sad she is. Where I come from, moves like that will get you an old-fashioned beat down, or worse."

"And what if she does something crazy like harm herself?" Pastor challenged. "I don't think I could live with that."

"Can you live without your wife and kids?"

"I really don't think it'll come to that," he argued.

His eyes intensified.

"What about your ministry?"

"This *is* part of my ministry."

"People are fickle," I interjected. "They can change loyalties in a heartbeat. I hope you know what you are doing."

Chapter 11

The second Zoe and I sat down across the table from Bob Wells at the deposition, I knew that it was going to be interesting. He had a rather big frame, much like a former athlete long past his prime. I could tell by his demeanor that he was angry at the very thought of having to be there. His round, bearded face was reddened, and his nostrils were flared, like a fire-breathing dragon. Angry people are never good witnesses— ever.

Scott Truman was the opposite. He was wearing a blue pinstriped suit with a solid red tie and dark-framed glasses, and he looked well-put-together. He was short with dark hair that looked like he had just gotten it cut that morning. He was approximately 50 years old.

Zoe was fidgety already. She wore a printed midi dress with flutter sleeves. Her curly hair was pinned up in the back. She was nervous while trying hard not to look directly at her perpetrator.

"Usual stipulations, Sam?" Scott asked.

"Yes," I replied.

Turning to the young female stenographer, he said, "Can you please note that for the record and swear the witness?"

"Do you swear under oath and penalty of law to tell the truth throughout this proceeding?"

"Yes, I do," the witness replied.

She nodded, and Scott gestured with his hand toward me to begin.

Q. Can you please state your full name for the record?

A. Robert Peter Wells

Q. Mr. Wells, how old are you?

A. I'm 40.

Q. Are you married?

A. Separated.

Q. What is your wife's name?

A. Rosanne.

Q. How can I find her? Where does she live?

A. Um… she lives in our house.

Q. And what is her address?

A. 303 Marlins Street, Utica.

Q. Do you have any children?

A. Two twin boys, age 16.

Q. How long have you worked at Longley Insurance Company?

A. Around ten years.

Q. What do you do there?

A. I'm a claims adjuster.

Q. Is that where you met my client, Zoe Carter?

A. Yes.

Q. Were you her supervisor?

A. Not exactly. She was a claims adjuster, too. I was just there a lot longer than she and I had seniority.

Q. Would you say she was a good worker?

A. Not exactly.

Q. What was the problem with her work?

A. Hard to say?

Q. Please try.

A. She spent too much time on the phone talking to her friends and family.

Q. Did you have to talk to her about it?

A. As I said, I wasn't her supervisor.

Q. Did anyone talk to her about the time she spent on the phone?

A. I don't know about that.

Q. Did you ever report to anyone that you thought she spent too much time on the phone on personal matters?

A. Me? No.

Q. Were there any other problems with her job performance that you were aware of?

A. Her attitude.

Q. How was her attitude?

A. Poor, I'd say.

Q. How was it poor?

A. She just complained a lot.

Q. Complained about what?

A. About corporate policy and procedures, you know.

Q. Was it a problem for you how she felt about corporate?

A. No, you asked me a question, and I answered it.

Q. Can you think of one specific policy or procedure that she complained to you about?

A. As I sit here now? Um, not really.

Q. Who were the other claims adjusters in the office with you two?

A. Mark Volpe and Cody Sinner.

Q. They would have had just as much opportunity as you did to observe Zoe's work and attitude, wouldn't you say?

A. How am I supposed to know what they observed?

Q. I'm sorry. I'm just asking if the four of you were there together in the office during the same time period?

A. Yeah, I guess that's right.

Q. So, if you were saying or doing anything inappropriate around Zoe, they may have seen or heard you do it?

A. I never did anything to her?

Q. Are you sure about that?

A. Yes.

Q. So you never touched her in an inappropriate manner?

A. No, never.

Q. Do you know what I mean by that?

A. Well… not exactly.

Q. So let me explain it to you. Did you ever try to touch Zoe on or about her breasts?

A. No.

Q. Did you ever try to touch Zoe on or about her backside?

A. No.

Q. On either hip?

A. No.

Q. On either shoulder.

A. No, I didn't.

Q. Did you ever try to rub your midsection or genitals up against Zoe Carter?

A. No, never.

Q. Did you ever intentionally adjust yourself in front of her?

A. No.

Q. Did you ever ask her out on a date?

A. I may have asked her one time if she wanted to go out for a drink, but that's all.

Q. Just the one time?

A. Yes.

Q. So there is no chance that Mark or Cody heard you or saw you do any of those things?

A. Again, I don't know what they supposedly saw or didn't. Mark was her boyfriend for a while. I saw them two together.

Q. You saw Mark Sinner and Zoe doing what exactly?

A. I don't know, flirting with each other.

Q. Did you ever talk to Mark about it?

A. No, but everybody knew that he liked her.

Q. Who is everybody?

A. I just meant Cody and I knew that something was going on?

Q. Were you jealous?

A. Me? Jealous. No way. [Laughter]

Q. But you liked her, too? Didn't you?

A. Not like you mean.

Q. But you just admitted to asking Zoe out for a date?

A. I am a married man.

Q. A married man who routinely cheated on your wife? Isn't that right?

A. What? How dare you!

Q. Who is Cheryl Walker?

A. Excuse me?

Q. Who is Cheryl Walker to you?

A. I'm not going to let you make this about me!

Q. You do understand that this is completely about you?

A. I never touched her! I already told you.

Q. How did you meet Miss Walker?

A. I'm not playing this game. No freakin way!

Q. Is this a game to you, Mr. Wells?

A. Go ahead, Zoe, tell them about all the stuff you routinely did with random guys!. Tell them about the abortion! You're sitting here acting like you're so innocent. Everybody knows what you really are!"

"I think we need a recess," Scott Truman spoke calmly into the brewing storm and stood to his feet.

He leaned over and whispered something in his client's ear, and Bob Wells rose, and the two men walked out of the room.

I turned to Zoe, who looked shell-shocked.

"Excuse me," the stenographer said. "I'm going to find the ladies' room."

She got up and walked out of the room.

"Zoe, you okay?"

"No," she replied. "I think I'm going to be sick."

She grabbed her stomach area with both hands and began breathing hard.

"Can I get you something? You want some water?"

She shook her head no.

"See, I knew he was going to do this," she fretted. "I tried to tell you."

"Yes, but it's all good for us," I said.

"*Good*? I'm shaking."

"Listen, we can't really talk here," I cautioned. "We can talk later. We just need to get through this today."

"Okay."

"Right now, it's important that you keep it together. You are doing great. I don't want this guy to see that he's getting to you."

"Okay, okay," she whispered.

Scott Truman suddenly reappeared with his client and the stenographer. He looked a lot more weathered than he had earlier. Bob Wells looked a mess as well, as he was covered in perspiration. He was obviously still angry.

I'm sorry, can you read back the last question?" I asked and looked at the stenographer.

Q. How did you meet Miss Walker?

A. She worked for us at my house.

Q. What kind of work did she do for you?

A. Housekeeping.

Q. And now you live with her, isn't that right?

A. No, not anymore.

Q. How long were the two of you together?

A. Two months.

Q. Where can I find her? Where does she live?

A. I don't know.

Q. You are not together anymore?

A. No.

Q. Who do you live with now?

A. Nobody. I live alone.

Q. Do you remember when Zoe filed a complaint against you with the Insurance Company?

A. Yes, I remember.

Q. Did someone from corporate reach out to talk to you

about it the way that they did Mark and Cody?

A. Yes. I talked to someone.

Q. Do you remember who that person was you spoke to?

A. No, I don't remember.

Q. Was it a man or a woman?

A. A man.

Q. Do you recall what you told him?

A. I told him that she was making everything up.

Q. Why do you think she was doing that?

A. I don't know. Ask her.

Q. I'm asking you, if you know.

A. I don't.

Q. So the two of you were on good terms?

A. Yeah, that is, until she went to corporate with her lies.

Q. What about before that?

A. Ah, I never had a problem with her.

Q. Ever have any problems with Mark or Cody?

A. No, them neither.

Q. Have you talked to either one of them about this lawsuit?

A. No, I haven't.

Q. Tell me about the Christmas party two years ago at Mama Mia's?

A. What about it?

Q. Didn't the manager throw you out of the restaurant because you grabbed a waitress in an inappropriate manner?

A. That's not how it happened!

Q. Please tell us how it did happen? Go ahead in your own words. We want to hear it.

A. No, I won't because none of this is relevant.

Q. It is relevant to whether you have a habit of getting handsy with women who you aren't married to. So, what happened that night? Explain it to us, please?

A. I told you that I'm not answering that.

Q. It's not up to you.

A. Oh, yes, it is!

Q. Do you want another break to talk to your attorney? We can wait.

A. No, I don't want to talk to this guy again. You and your client can go to hell for all I care! How about that? I know a setup when I see one. This is over!

The witness jumped to his feet, hissed like a wild cat toward Scott Truman, and shot me a dirty look. The rest of us just watched in silence as he stormed out, mumbling expletives to himself. Neither one of us moved right away.

"Let the record reflect that the witness has left the room prior to the completion of the deposition," I finally said.

Chapter 12

It took a while for me to really get to know Carla's father. We were very different, and it took a minute for me to get past his conservative worldview. One thing that I can say is that he never pretended to be anyone he wasn't. He was unlike any Black man that I had ever met before. But he obviously loved his daughter very much, which was all I really cared about. I decided that I respected him.

He put the nursery furniture together and put the drapes up without any help from me, which was a big relief. I always meant to do it, but I just couldn't seem to find the time. I heard what Carla said before, and I was really trying not to burn the candle at both ends. Also, I wasn't much of a handyman, so it was going to take me even that much longer to put two cribs together.

"So, how did I do?" Mr. Jenkins asked.

He leaned back with both hands on his hips, admiring his handiwork.

"It looks great!" I complimented.. "It really does. I can't thank you enough."

"You don't have to thank me. There is nothing too good for my grandchildren. Remember that!"

"I got it," I said.

"Do you want me to bring down the drapes a little lower? I wasn't exactly sure how you wanted them."

"No, that is good. I can't believe how easy it was for you to get them up. I was dreading the thought of getting up on that ladder."

"I worked at a hardware store for a while when I was in college," he revealed. "I somehow managed to learn a thing or two."

"Well, I have never really been that good with my hands."

"Sam, I know that you never had a father yourself and you're probably a little nervous about everything, but I want you to know that I think you're going to be a terrific father."

"I hope so," I mouthed.

"I know so," he emphasized. "Like I said at your wedding, you are everything that I could have ever wanted for my daughter."

"Thanks."

"You know, it turned out that being a father was the most natural thing that I have ever done. Much easier than being a husband— by a long shot."

"Honestly, I was thinking just the opposite," I admitted. "Loving Carla is easy for me. I can't really explain it. But I think I'm going to have to figure out this being a dad stuff. Everything about it seems so... I don't know."

"Just feel your way through," he advised. "And try not to overthink it. Babies grow inside their mothers, so there is already that connection there before they are even born. But obviously that's not the case for us guys. Sometimes it takes time to build that connection. But let me tell you something, it's the best feeling that I have ever known."

"I'm just having a hard time seeing myself doing it," I divulged. "My sisters are just a couple of years younger than I am. I have never really been around infants, that I can remember."

"It's like riding a bike. You'll see."

"Everybody keeps saying that," I said. "All my dreams came true when I married your daughter. I'm not sure now that I ever really wanted anything more. Carla has always wanted to be a mom. So, this is really her dream, not mine."

"Sounds to me like it's time for you to dream bigger," he insisted.

"*Bigger*?"

"There's always bigger," he stressed.

"I'm not so sure that bigger is always better."

"You are just gonna have to trust me with this one," he said and grinned.

I just looked at him.

"Sam, show me a man without a dream, and I'll show you somebody who is just waiting to die. That's not you, man."

He patted me softly on the back twice and turned and walked out of the nursery.

———•●•———

Pauline Carter called me at the office. It was right before 5:00 o'clock, and I was a little bothered because I was planning to leave on time today. Carla had given me a list of things that she wanted me to go out and buy and bring up to her at the hospital. Nothing against Mrs. Carter, but if she had any questions about what happened at the deposition yesterday, then she should talk to her daughter. It's just easier that way.

"Thank you for taking my call," she said.

"Oh, it's nothing," I replied. "Is there a problem?"

"I was wondering if it would be possible for me to make an appointment to come in and speak to you?"

"Can I ask why you want to see me?"

"Zoe was really upset after what happened yesterday," she said. "Good thing you cancelled her deposition today, because there is no way that she would have been able to handle that. I think I have some information that might make things a little clearer for you."

"I don't know what she told you, but I don't think that it could have gone any better for us yesterday."

"Yes, I know," she said. "But I still think that it's important that we speak… privately."

"Okay, when do you want to come in?"

"My schedule is pretty open, so you tell me."

"Is tomorrow too soon?" I wondered.

"No, what time?"

"Can you do 1 o'clock?"

"Yes, I can. Thank you."

"All right, I will see you then,"

I had no idea why she needed to speak to me. We didn't exactly cancel Zoe's deposition. I told Scott Truman that he couldn't take Zoe's testimony until Bob Wells came back to let me finish with him. I wasn't in any hurry to move this case along.

I gathered my stuff and rushed out as soon as I hung up the phone with Zoe's mother. I spent the morning in Utica

City Court waiting for the judge to call my case, which was just a simple DWI. In my opinion, it took much longer than was necessary. The long delay put me behind in my other work, which left me feeling anxious.

For the first stop, I needed to go to the mall to get Carla some fancy lotion and makeup that she wanted. I was worried about the traffic. I also needed to get to the dry cleaners before it closed and then pick up something for myself for dinner. I thought through the most efficient route to get everything done. The more time that I spent running around town, the less time that I could spend with my wife.

I was leaving the dry cleaners when I remembered that Carla also wanted me to pick up the new Essence Magazine. I was in the process of making a U-turn when I broke out in a ridiculous sweat, and my heart began racing. I had no idea what was happening. It felt like someone had poured a bucket of water on my head. I was panting a little because I found it a little hard to breathe.

Fortunately, I somehow managed to safely pull over to the side of the road, and I sat there for several minutes trying to regain my composure. I cleaned myself up as best I could, ran into the supermarket to get the magazine, and drove home. I was glad that none of my in-laws were there to see the state that I was in. I took a quick shower, ate a bowl of breakfast cereal, and rushed out the door to go and see my bride.

"Sorry, I'm so late," I uttered.

"You're not late," she said. "How was your day?"

"Good. I got everything on your list."

I put the small bag down on the table next to the bed.

"Thank you. Did you eat dinner?

"Yeah."

"What did you have?"

"Just a little something at the house," I fudged. "I was rushing to get here."

"Um, I saw my doctor today."

"What did he say? Do we have a date?"

"Thursday."

"The day after tomorrow?"

"Uh huh."

"At thirty-four weeks?" I questioned.

"Yeah."

"Wow!"

"I know," she uttered. "Can you believe it?"

"Did you tell your mother?"

"Yes, they are coming over tomorrow night."

"What time on Thursday?"

"Uh, he just said in the morning."

"Wow."

"What are you thinking?" she pressed.

"I don't know. Are you ready for this?"

"I'm ready for this part to be over, that's for sure," she said.

"Me too," I agreed.

"Sam, can you believe that we are about to become the parents of twins?"

"No," I admitted. "What on earth have we done?"

"It's too late to be asking that question, don't you think?" she questioned. "The babies are coming whether we like it or not."

"I know that," I defended. "I'm not worried. God has got this."

"How can you be so sure?" she asked with a clear tremble in her voice.

"Because He told me so. That's how I know."

"Okay, if you say so," she acquiesced.

"I do."

She looked deep into my eyes for a quick second.

"Can you get me that?" she asked.

I reached over and handed her the bag that I had just brought in, and she immediately began fishing through it.

"What's this?" she asked.

"What does it look like?"

"I didn't ask you for nail polish."

"I know," I replied. "I just thought you would like it for your toes."

"My *toes*?" she asked and started laughing hard."

I shrugged my shoulders.

"I told you that I can barely see my toes," she scolded. "I'm not sure that I will ever see them again."

"Sure, you will," I encouraged.

"You like this color then?"

"Yes, it's called *passion red*," I replied. "It reminded me of you."

"Really?"

"You don't like it?" I asked.

"No, I do," she stated. "I was just wondering how you think about such things."

———•●•———

I escorted Zoe's mother to my office. She was wearing a tan trench coat. For some reason, she was taller than I remembered, more athletic-looking.

"Is it raining out?" I wondered.

"Yes, but it's supposed to stop soon."

"I'm inside all day on most days, and a hurricane could be happening, and I wouldn't have a clue. Please have a seat."

"Thank you," she said.

She was nervous and uncomfortable in the way that Zoe was during the deposition. They had similar mannerisms, something else that I had missed before.

"I didn't know that you are married to Carla Jenkins from the news," she said.

"Yes, we've been married just over a year now."

"I always thought she was so beautiful and elegant."

"Thank you. How can I help you, Mrs. Carter?"

"Well, my daughter was very upset after hearing Bob Wells testify."

"Yes, I know."

"I guess he tried to make her sound like a loose woman or something."

"He can say whatever he wants," I replied. "Doesn't make it true."

"I need to tell you something that happened to Zoe when she was in high school."

My heart sank because I feared that I already knew what she was going to say based on what happened to Carla when she was in high school. I quickly braced myself.

"Okay," I mouthed.

"We raised her right, and she was always a good girl," she began. "But she struggled a lot in school on account of being one of the few Black kids in the entire school district.

She never felt like she fit in completely. I guess all girls struggle a little, so I'm not making excuses, but it was hard for her a lot."

"I understand."

"One night after a high school football game, she was doing something with this boy from school, whom she barely knew, and ended up getting pregnant. Fortunately, she told me right away, and I took care of it."

She had a determined look on her face, and there was some weight to every word she spoke. This was a strong woman, I could tell.

"What do you mean?" I questioned.

"I took her to get an abortion."

"I see."

"And we never told anyone at the time," she added.

"Okay."

"I mean, no one, not even her father," she emphasized.

"Oh...okay, but then how does Bob Wells know about it?"

"Zoe has a lot of guilt about it, and I guess she confided in the wrong person," she surmised. "I have tried to tell her to get over it and just move on with her life, but she won't... or can't. She was 16 years old and already going through a pretty hard time... Being big pregnant for the entire world to see and judge her would have sent her over the deep end for good. I know that for a fact... I couldn't let her go through that— no way! We did what was best for everyone, and I would make the same choice again if I had to."

"Okay, so what do you want me to do now?" I questioned.

"I just don't think that Zoe is going to be able to go

through with the trial. Joe is the one who wanted all of this in the first place. He never really listens."

"But it sounds like he doesn't have all of the facts."

"He knows enough," she contended. "He knows how fragile she is."

"There is no trial scheduled," I explained. "For what it's worth, I think that there's a pretty good chance that the Insurance Company is going to offer Zoe some kind of a settlement?"

"How much?" she wondered.

"I have no idea how much, but they are generally too risk-averse to take a chance at going to trial and losing big."

"I pray that we do settle this because if there is a trial and this Bob Wells starts talking about the abortion again… my husband will… he is going to have a heart attack."

"Maybe you should tell him then," I suggested. "I'm not judging you, but it's a pretty big secret. I know that I would feel betrayed if I were him."

"The truth is that we have never been good at our communication," she articulated. "I have found out things, too, about him that I just had to get over."

"Hmm."

"Joe grew up catholic," she continued. "I don't know if I even believe in God or religion. It seems… I don't know what I'm trying to say. But I only agreed to have Zoe baptized in the church to make him happy. He's really only religious in a surface kind of way, if you know what I mean. He doesn't go to church or support it in any way. But he has opinions based on how he was raised that I don't necessarily agree with."

I didn't know what I was supposed to say, so I just

remained silent. She came to see me to tell me something specific about Zoe, not to hear my judgment. I felt bad for her and her family.

"Joe loves Zoe, but he has never really tried to know or understand her," she alleged. "She resents him for it."

"And you? Do you resent him?"

She rubbed her hands on her thighs and looked away.

"I'm very sorry, but isn't he going to find out eventually?" I questioned.

"I guess I'll deal with that when it happens," she argued. "Zoe is still my main concern now. Joe has three other children from his first marriage. I only have her."

"Sounds to me like your daughter is in a lot of pain."

"I think she's drinking too much," Mrs. Carter disclosed. "I don't know what else she is doing. I'm worried to death about her. I probably made a mistake not trying to get her some help before now."

"I know it's hard loving people," I said. "We are all so broken."

Chapter 13

Carla didn't want a lot of people to know that she was being induced. I only told Pastor Justin and Mama, of course. Her immediate family was all there, including Christina and her brother Christopher. I know that they were all a little nervous, but the overall mood was light. This was a joyous occasion after all.

Christopher was funny, and he knew better than anyone how to irritate his sisters.

"That's not funny!" Carla rebuked. "You are not supposed to say anything about any woman's weight, especially not when she's pregnant. What's wrong with you?"

"Ah, I didn't say anything," he replied. "You *do* look a little like a linebacker on a junior high football team. It's not a bad thing. People love football."

"You need to hush up," Carla directed.

I knew almost everything about her, so obviously, I knew that she was terrified. And she knew that I was aware of her inner struggles. But she hid it well, and I was proud of her. We had agreed to present a united front and to battle through this attack together— as one flesh.

"Sam, is your grandmother coming this morning?" Mrs. Jenkins asked.

"No, I told her that we don't know how long the labor will last, and she'll just be looking at the four walls in the waiting room. She'll probably come this afternoon."

The idle talk was a poor distraction. All of the waiting around was weighing heavily on me. I wished that they would just get the induction started, because I was getting anxious. I was also thinking that I needed to keep it together emotionally so as not to have another episode like I had two just days ago. I wanted to be there for Carla, and I didn't want to do anything that might disqualify me from being with her.

We were all huddled together in her room for about two hours before the two nurses came to get her. Everyone said their goodbyes, and Carla and I were taken to another room. She was given the drug through her IV. I held her hand, and we waited.

There were several people in and out of the room regularly checking the monitors and keeping an eye on her. Honestly, I was glad about that because it seemed like they were on top of everything. I felt like my prayers had already been answered in that Carla was getting to deliver naturally.

The first real contraction caused her entire body to shake uncontrollably. She immediately screamed out in pain, the intensity of which shook me to my core. One or more of the machines began beeping incessantly. All of my senses were suddenly on overload, and I wasn't able to fully process all that was happening in the room. I just remember a lot of people rushing in, and some guy getting in my face and telling me that I had to leave. I'm not sure if I resisted him in any way, but it wouldn't surprise me if I did.

I have no idea what I looked like, but I must have looked pretty bad when I walked into the waiting room because Carla's mom took one look at me, and she let out a scream. Remarkably, it was her reaction that brought me crashing back to reality. I somehow managed to explain to them what just happened, and in so doing, elevated the tension in the room to a boiling point.

"So, what did they say exactly?" Christina asked.

"Nothing to me. They just told me that I had to wait here."

"Was she conscious?"

"She was in pain and shaking."

"You mean like a seizure?" she pressed.

"I don't know."

"If they gave her Pitocin, like they did me, and she reacted like that, then they have to do a C-section?"

"She didn't want a C-section," I said.

"It's not up to her," Christina explained. "They probably should have done this in the first place. I was worried about this."

"About what?" Mr. Jenkins asked.

"Her body has already been through a lot, especially with all of the blood pressure medications. I get that vaginal delivery is best for most women, but it just seemed too risky in this situation."

"How come you didn't say anything?" Mr. Jenkins wondered.

"I'm just a nurse," Carla replied. "He's a doctor who specializes in this, who knows more than I do."

Nobody said anything in response, and we spoke

infrequently over the next two hours. It was sobering for me sitting there, lost in confusion. I tried to pray quietly to myself, but kept running out of words. I kept having to start over again. My growing fear was slowly tightening its grip on me and my mind like a giant python, and even though I knew it was demonic in origin and should be silenced, it was getting harder to ignore. Eventually, I just gave up on the idea of praying altogether and instead opted to try to rest my mind by turning down the haunting voices inside my head.

"Sam," Dr. O'Connor spoke.

The five of us jumped to attention in unison as if we were young children playing a round of musical chairs. Under different circumstances, it might have been comical.

He was a dark-haired man of average height with a thin frame. He appeared to be in his 50s, and he was dressed in light blue scrubs. He walked in the midst of us and faced me. I thought he looked tired as he rubbed his red eyes.

"Carla delivered the babies by emergency C-section," he began. "Her liver enzymes were quite high, and the fetal heart rates dropped considerably. Baby #1, a girl, weighed 3 lbs. 2 oz., and Baby #2, a boy, weighed in at 2 lbs. 6 oz. They have both been taken to the Neonatal Intensive Care Unit (NICU) for hypoglycemia and jaundice, which are common for babies born prematurely. Although we can't be certain, there doesn't appear to be any other complications with either one of them at this point."

"What is hypoglycemia?" Mrs. Jenkins inquired.

"It's a blood glucose level below the normal range. Premature babies generally have immature glucose regulation systems."

"Is it dangerous?"

"It can be, but no, not generally."

He was looking like he was quickly losing energy himself. It was obvious that he wasn't enjoying the moment.

"How's my wife?" I blurted out with such force that it startled everyone.

"Um… she experienced some organ failure in her kidneys and liver, which we don't know the extent of. She was hemorrhaging a bit, and frankly, it was touch and go there for a while."

"But she's going to be all right?" I interjected and held my breath.

"It's too early to say. She's being moved to intensive care, and it's going to be a while until we know the extent of the organ damage. She's in critical condition."

"Oh my god!" Mrs. Jenkins exclaimed, and grabbed her husband by the arm, and buried her face.

"Is she conscious?" Christina asked.

"No."

"She's in a coma?" Christina continued.

"Yes, medically induced and intubated."

"Did she have a seizure?" she followed up.

"Most likely."

"So, she could have brain damage?"

"Yes, maybe."

"I don't understand why you aren't saying more?" Christina expressed. "We just want to know everything that's going on with my sister. Just tell us!"

"I'm sorry," the doctor offered. "I know it's frustrating. Believe me, we are doing everything that we can for her, and I'm consulting with experts in severe preeclampsia from other hospitals. At this point, all we can do is wait and see how she responds."

"How long before we know more definitely?" Christina demanded.

"Hard to say," he answered. "Her numbers are all over the place, and we need to get her stabilized. Like I already said, it's way too early to tell too much. She needs time to recover from the extensive trauma to her body. She's a very sick woman, I'm sorry to have to say."

"Can I see her?" I begged.

"Yes, I'll tell them. Anything else?"

"Can we see the babies?" Christina asked.

"Tomorrow in the NICU."

I was in a daze, like a punch-drunk boxer going down for the third time. I watched Carla's family immediately circle together and comfort one another. Christopher was sobbing, and Christina was holding on to him. I felt out of place, like I somehow didn't belong there with them, and I stepped a few feet away, sat down, and stared at the floor. I was content to focus again on my breathing. I have no idea how long I sat there like that.

"Sam!" Mama called out.

"Yes," I answered instinctively without moving.

"Sam, what happened?"

I looked her in the eye, and I tried to answer her, but the words wouldn't come out. It was weird. I knew what I wanted to say, but the words kept disappearing from the screen of my mind when I tried to verbalize them. I was left a befuddled mess, like a frightened little boy awakening from a nightmare— except that this wasn't a dream.

She turned and walked away. I heard them talking behind me, and I blocked out their conversation like it was benign elevator music. I went back into my dark cave.

"Here, drink this," Mama demanded.

I followed her direction without hesitation. It was lukewarm water.

"It's all gonna be okay," she whispered calmly. "Carla is gonna be just fine, just you wait and see."

I had little more than a spark of hope. Not all of the voices in my head were bad ones; however, it's just that fear in the heart will always try to be the lead singer and drown out the other voices. I was listening for the right song with lyrics that lined up with scripture and what I already knew to be true about God, that is, that He is an ever-present help in our time of need. So once again, the real battlefield was in my mind.

The ICU nurse said that only two people could go in to see Carla at a time. In hindsight, I should have gone in first by myself. But Carla's mom wanted to come in with me. As wonderful a woman as she was, she didn't know the Lord, at least not the way that I did. She carried her burdens alone, which meant that she was like dead weight to me in that moment.

As soon as we walked into the room and saw Carla lying lifeless attached to machines, Mrs. Jenkins let out a loud groan, rushed to the bedside, and started begging her daughter to wake up.

"Carla, honey, I need you to wake up! Open your eyes! It's me! Mom and I love you with all of my heart. I know that you can do it. You're my angel baby. C'mon sweetheart! Just wake up now. Please baby! Beautiful girl."

I gently stroked my mother-in-law's shoulder as she continued to pour out her heart with reckless abandon. Her face was covered in tears, and she was unsteady on her feet. We had been sitting together in the waiting room for hours just ruminating on all of the possible scenarios, and now her pain and fear gushed out together in utter desperation. She emoted there for several minutes before slowly running out of steam. She turned and fell into my arms, and I held her tight.

"Go get Chris," I finally whispered.

"Okay," she said through her tears. "I'll go get him. I'll be right back."

I watched her walk slowly out of the room. I figured I had just a couple of minutes before she returned with her husband, so I needed to act quickly.

"Carla," I softly whispered. "You did it! I don't know if they told you, but you are a mother now... It's what you always wanted... We've got two babies— a boy and a girl! You did it! I am so proud of you. I knew that you could do it... And I know how tired you are now. You just need to rest so that we can all go home together as a family... Take your time. I'm not going anywhere... If you get lost, just listen for my voice and no one else's, and I will show you the way out... Just follow me. God said He will pull us through... I'd never lie about that. I know that you believe me.... I'll be right here when you wake up. I promise. Now... now you sleep."

———•●•———

I slowly opened my eyes. It felt like I had been hit by a Mack truck. It took a couple of seconds before I remembered where I was... and the rest of it. The clock on the wall read

5:03 a.m. One of the nurses had kindly brought me some pillows, and I had propped them up in a way that allowed me to doze. I never fell into a real sleep because the nurse was in and out of the room a lot.

My back hurt, and my left leg was aching. Ever since I was injured two years ago, my leg would often give me a little bit of a problem, especially if I slept on my left side. I suddenly realized that I was also hungry. Mama had gotten me a ham sandwich from the cafeteria and some coffee. That's all that I had to eat all day. I had only left Carla's room once to go to the bathroom.

I peeked over at Carla, and she was still sleeping. I made everyone go home at 9:00 o'clock when visiting hours ended. I refused to leave, and the nurse said that she had gotten permission for me to stay. I mostly just sat there and watched over her like a bodyguard. A couple of times, I adjusted the blankets and kissed her face. She never moved or made a sound.

At 9:00 a.m. sharp, Carla's mom walked into the room. She had clearly showered and changed her clothes and looked good considering everything.

"How's Carla?"

"The same," I replied and sat up straight in the chair.

I felt like a hundred-year-old man.

She walked over to the bed and gazed down lovingly at Carla for a few seconds.

"Ah, Sam, everyone is here," she advised. "We are going to have a family meeting now in the waiting room before other people get here and take over that space."

"Okay," I said. "I'll just be here."

"No, honey, you don't understand," she said.

She looked at me sweetly.

"No, I'm not going anywhere," I resisted. "You guys can talk without me. I don't need anything. Really, I'm good."

She walked over to me and got down on her knees before me. Her eyes were heavy with emotion, like a storm cloud during the calm. She then took both of my hands in her hands and looked me deeply in my eyes.

"Sam, honey, listen to me please," she began. "I know how much you love Carla. Frankly, the whole world knows it... Honestly, I have never seen any man love a woman this hard before. I didn't think it was possible... Between us, I have never been jealous of any woman before in my life, but I envy my daughter this one thing. It's truly amazing! But right now, she needs everyone who loves the two of you to come together and come up with a game plan that works for everyone, especially for you! Please, can we do this?"

"...Okay...maybe... but just for a minute," I reluctantly agreed.

I felt put upon.

She stood to her feet and offered me her hand. I took it, and we walked to the waiting room together. I was so tired. My body was screaming out in pain with each step, which I quickly ignored. It was easy. In the back of my mind, I was still thinking that this was an interruption that I could have done without.

It felt like an ambush as soon as we walked into the waiting room. In addition to Carla's immediate family and Mama, also present was her Uncle Sheldon from Rochester, who officiated our wedding, and his wife. Christina's husband, Eric, was there too, along with Pastors Justin and

Marlene. They were silent as I took the *hot seat* that was offered to me.

"Okay, everyone is here," Mrs. Jenkins announced, her mission accomplished.

"Sam, was there any change overnight?" Christina asked.

"No," I answered abruptly without looking at her.

"Oh, all right," she reacted. "First, I think that we should come up with a schedule for being here at the hospital. At least initially, I think someone should be here with Carla 24/7."

"I agree," Chris said.

"I'll be here," I proclaimed. "I got it covered."

"But you can't be here all the time," Christina asserted.

"Why not?" I challenged.

"Oh, Sam! You're going to completely burn yourself out! You need to go home now and get some rest. We don't know how long… how long before Carla… how long she is going to be here."

"You think that she is going to die, don't you!" I attacked. "Is that it?"

"I uh, I never said that," Christina defended.

Her eyes were big, and she was clutching her chest with both hands.

"But that's what you think, isn't it?" I unleashed. "And I'm telling you that she's not going to die. She is going to wake up any second, and I need to be here when she does. Then we're going to take our babies home and be a family. We promised each other."

"Sam, everyone here believes that too," Carla's uncle interjected. "It's just that in the meantime, we need to do what we know to do in the natural, while we are waiting for God to move in his perfect timing. You need help, son! Let us help you!"

"Think about the babies," Christina said.

"I am thinking about the babies," I insisted. "They need their mother."

"You're right, they do," Christina agreed. "But they are fighting too. They're not fully developed, and they face all kinds of complications, including infection and breathing issues."

"Then how about this?" I posed. "You all look out for the babies, and I'll stay with Carla. How's that for a plan?"

Everyone was silent. I was fuming inside, which surprisingly gave me energy and a reprieve from striving all night.

"Excuse me, everyone," Pastor Justin spoke up. "But I need to speak to Sam alone. We are going to take a short walk, and we'll be right back. Please excuse us."

Pastor stood to his feet and came over to me. I was seated with my head down. I didn't move.

"Let's go, Sam," he directed.

"I looked up at him in a glance and begrudgingly stood to my feet. There was a small storm brewing inside me, and I embraced it. I was mad at the whole world again, a feeling that I used to love and embrace like an old lover.

We didn't say a word as we walked toward the elevator. He pushed the button, and we waited without making eye contact. Down deep, I knew that I was acting like a child, but I didn't care. I just wanted these people to leave me alone.

We got in the elevator, and he pushed the button again. We got off on the first floor, walked down the long hall toward the main entrance, and left through the main doors. My head was still in a bit of a fog. It was all that I could do to put one foot in front of the other.

The cool fall morning air hit me and felt good against my face. I breathed it in hard like it was perfume, and it woke me up from my stupor. I yawned big, and my jaw cracked. I had a major league headache.

We walked down a path that led to what looked like some kind of storage facility. There was no one else in the vicinity, except a woman walking a small dog in the distance.

"Now, tell me what is going on with you?" Pastor solicited.

"I don't know what you mean," I fought.

"Yes, you do," he insisted.

"I'm tired."

"What else?"

"I'm angry."

"Angry?"

"Yes, I'm angry that this is happening to us."

"Are you angry at God?"

I don't know," I answered truthfully.

"We've all been there, brother," Pastor pointed out. "I know I have. I told you some of it. It's normal."

"I don't feel normal."

"But you are," he maintained. "Nobody said it would be easy."

"I think that I have met my match," I complained. "This might be more than I can bear."

"Then why won't you let anyone help you?"

"Because nobody can …help me," I insisted.

"You don't know that."

"Yes, I do!"

"Everybody needs everybody else," he presented. "God made us that way. No lone rangers because it's impossible to grow in our knowledge of Him that way."

"Grow in what?" I challenged. "I don't care about that."

"I see."

"No, you don't! You couldn't possibly know…"

"Then tell me."

"This is all my fault," I spoke freely. "Don't you see? Carla is in there fighting for her life because of me!"

"What are you talking about?"

"We men have it easy when it comes to bringing life into this world. But it's the women who bear all of the pain and risk their lives."

"Every man who has ever loved a woman feels that way, regardless of whether we admit it or not," Pastor argued. "But we can't change nature."

"This guilt is like nothing I have ever felt before," I confessed. "It's got a stranglehold on me, and I can barely see straight when… I look at her family, especially her mom… Those people don't deserve any of this. Carla doesn't deserve to be…Tell me, what am I supposed to do with that?"

"Be a husband and a father to the kids the two of you created together and brought into the world. Both are lifetime commitments, and it evens out in the end. I promise you."

"I wish that I could trade places with her. I'd gladly do it."

"Nobody is blaming you," Pastor Justin argued. "All

those people waiting in there love you both, and you are pushing them away. "

"I don't care about any of that," I responded.

"Sam, it's time to get over yourself and your broken emotions."

"I'm sorry, but I don't know how to do that," I declared. "I'm only human. I'm just flesh and blood."

"But with a born-again spirit inside that's incorruptible and infinite," Pastor added. "Act like it for the love of God!"

"So, what do you think I should do?" I implored. "I'm so tired. Just tell me what you want me to do!"

"Like the pastor just said to you in that room, you do your part and let God do His. Either you trust Him, or you don't. And if you trust Him, then rise above your private pain and act like you do. Sam, it's really as simple as that."

"*Simple*?" I reacted. "Really?"

"*Simple* doesn't necessarily mean *easy*," he suggested. "It just means that something is plain to see. It's the doing part that is often hard to accomplish. The Gospel of Jesus is *simple*."

I was silently thinking.

"So, what do you think?" he inquired. "You ready to do this?"

"No," I quickly answered, unable to hide my trepidation. "I'm not even close to ready."

"That's the thing, none of us are ever really ready to face the unknown," he pronounced. "That's what makes it a fight."

He nodded his head toward the hospital with a sly grin. I inhaled deeply and slowly let the clean air exit through my mouth. Together, in unison, we both turned around and headed back down the path toward the main entrance to the hospital. Suddenly, both my body and my soul were chilled.

———•⬤•———

"Um, listen everyone," I said as soon as I walked into the room. "I'm very sorry for the way I acted before. I have no excuse. I just hope that you can forgive me."

"What do you mean you don't have any excuse?" Mama refuted. "From where I'm standing, you have every excuse in the world to be just as ornery as you want to be. That's *your* wife they got in there attached to all those machines. This would break any man. So, you forget about it. The hell with anyone who thinks any difference."

"I agree with her," Christina spoke through a trembling voice on the brink of giving out. "It must have felt a like we were ganging up on you, and I assure you that was not my intention at all. Sam, I'm so sorry."

"You don't have to apologize to me," I replied. "I don't mind telling you that I don't have a clue what I'm doing. And I do want you all to know that I know that I can't do this by myself. The only thing I ask is that you bear with me. It might not look like it, but I really am trying."

"How about this, Sam?" Chris said. "Let's start over with you telling us what you need from us."

"…Um, I don't want Carla to be alone for long. I am going to stay here all night every night until she wakes up."

"So, that means that you can't be here during the day because you have to go home and sleep," he offered.

"I'm going to be here every day, so I can sit with her," Mrs. Jenkins said.

"The rest of us can fill in the gap so that you guys don't get too tired," Christina interjected.

"The church can provide meals so that you all don't have to worry about cooking or shopping," Pastor Marlene said.

"Oh, thank you!" Mrs. Jenkins reacted. "That is so kind."

"It's nothing, really," Pastor replied. "I have a whole team of ladies who are anxious to do it."

"All right, I think that's a pretty good start," Christina said. "We will just have to figure the rest of it out as we go. Sam, can you think of anything else?"

"… No, not really… but … there is maybe this one thing...

"What is it, son?" Chris asked.

"It's important to me that when you are with Carla, you keep it really positive. I think she knows what is going on and that she can hear us. So, be careful to encourage her with your words and keep it upbeat. She needs to feel your love and know that she is supported."

"Okay," Chris replied. "I think that we can all do that."

"Just bless her, don't beg her," I added. "That's all I got."

Everyone nodded in agreement, followed by an awkward silence.

"Well said, Sam," Pastor Jenkins spoke. "I think it's important for all of us, me included, to keep in mind now, more than ever, that we are united together in this struggle against the devil and that we keep our faith fully engaged. God can do all things; we know he can! So, we have to hold on to the idea that Carla is going to fully recover until we know definitively otherwise. Pastor Justin, do you mind praying over our family?"

"Not at all," Pastor replied and sat straight up and bowed his head.

Heavenly Father, we come boldly into your throne room of

grace. We know that you are the all-powerful, all-knowing God.

That you are good and that you give strength to all. Father,

right now, I pray that you touch this precious family in a special way. Let them each feel your presence in a new way and show them your glory. Draw them closer to you and let them come to know you for who you are. Rain down your blessing and save them. Father God, we ask that you manifest your healing power in Carla and in the two babies that you have given to them as an inheritance. Our hope and our trust is in you, Lord and that's why, even in our hour of need, we bless your name. Thank you for everything that you have done for us, and for what you are about

to do. In Jesus' name we pray. Amen.

Chapter 14

As I looked down upon Carla lying there still in critical condition, so many random and idle thoughts ran rampant through my mind like trains running in and out of Grand Central Station. I was reminded of our tortured journey to find each other. We had already been through so much with the breakup and the stabbing, not to mention all of our personal baggage that we both carried from our youth. The fact is that I was finally convinced that we had basically made it to the Promised Land, and we were anxiously looking forwarding to spending the rest of our lives together living in the overflow of God's grace and tender mercies, which are new every day.

It poured rain on our wedding day. Carla's mom took it as a personal affront by God and the angels after her many months of planning and obsessing. Although we couldn't show it, Carla and I thought it was funny. We were just so ready for all of the formalities to be over and for the rest of our lives together to begin.

Interestingly, rain on your wedding day is supposed to be good luck because rain represents nurturing the land and symbolizes the fertility of the couple and the abundance of the children to come— or so they say. Regardless, we did have an outdoor rain plan, so no one really got that wet.

I know that every groom feels this way, but Carla was the most beautiful woman in the world to me, and she looked simply stunning walking down the aisle toward me. She wore a white, hand-embroidered lace ball gown with cap sleeves, a drop waist, and a mock-neckline. I began crying the second I first saw her.

Unlike Christina and Eric, who were married in a fancy downtown hotel ballroom, we were married in a church, which was the only thing that I insisted on. I wanted a place where the Holy Spirit could feel welcomed and be fully present to anoint our love. And He showed up big for us!

Mrs. Jenkins scoured Wayne County for months, looking for just the right church that lived up to *her* vision for her daughter's wedding. Ultimately, she found a picturesque Methodist church in Sodus Point, New York, that looked like a piece of paradise. Christopher and Christina stood up with us. The entire wedding felt like we were in a magical glitter snow globe. All I heard in my ears all day long was melodies from heaven.

But time has a way of passing like pages in a good book. I never imagined that things could change for the worse so drastically— almost overnight. I made a promise to myself that when we got through this trial, I would never take the good times for granted again.

The babies were two days old, and I still hadn't seen them yet. Mrs. Jenkins told me that they were beautiful… and so small and delicate. I figured that everyone in the family had probably already visited them in the NICU at least once, except for me. I wasn't ready yet. I wanted to wait for Carla so that we could meet our children together.

The good news was that the doctor said that her vitals were no longer dropping and had stabilized somewhat. But there still wasn't much more that he could tell us, including how much longer she would be in this condition. It was all so draining on every level— physically, emotionally, and spiritually.

In response to a question from Christina, Dr. O'Connor refused to speculate on her chances of survival or making a full recovery. I resented the question, which I interpreted as being negative. But I wisely didn't say anything, Although, Mama was right that I should be given some deference because Carla was my wife; other people loved her too. They also deserved some grace and to have their questions about her condition answered.

I watched Carla like a hawk every second that I was there — just looking for any sign whatsoever that she was waking up. Being on guard like that was very tiring in itself. It felt a little like it did when I was trying a case in court. It was important to me that I not miss a thing. In my eyes, she was getting stronger with every breath.

Mama brought me dinner one afternoon at the hospital and set it up in the waiting room. She made all of my favorite foods— collard greens, macaroni salad, and fried chicken, all of which she had packed up and transported on the bus. It smelled delicious. Although I really didn't want it, I ate most of it as she sat next to me and encouraged me gently without saying a word.

I knew we weren't alone in this battle for our lives. I knew that people cared a lot about us and were praying hard for us. But much like fans at a sporting event cheering for their favorite team, their support could only go so far. In the end, the athletes on the field are the ones who have to actually play the game… before the time runs out.

Ultimately, I came to realize that no part of our living in this broken world we call reality is truly paradise. The war is still raging, and there are new battles every day — for everyone. So, regardless of what happened, I wasn't losing this fight or giving up hope.

— • ● • —

"Ah, Sam?" Mrs. Jenkins said when I was sitting at the kitchen table, rushing through the meatloaf dinner that she had kindly heated up for me, and insisted that I eat before heading off to the hospital.

"Yes."

"Did you and Carla ever come up with names for the babies?"

"Um…no, not really," I replied. "We were working on it."

"Well, the nurse told me that they are going to ask you," she advised. "They apparently need to know."

"Did they say why they needed to know now?"

"No, but I think that it would be good too, you know—better than calling them '*Baby A*' and '*Baby B*.' Don't you think?"

"Okay. Thanks for letting me know," I replied.

I quickly put my head down. I didn't want to waste any more time talking about things that didn't matter. There was some important place that I really needed to be.

I knew in the moment that I was being perceived as

unnecessarily difficult by everyone and that they were all reluctant to approach me with any of their concerns. And I freely acknowledged that they had a point and that I was probably missing the mark in many ways. But I was trying, I swear that I was.

No doubt, Carla would have had issues with the way that I was behaving. However, in my mind, I needed to stay focused on the right things or else we weren't going to make it out of this hell. At that point, Carla was my whole life, not the babies, who I didn't even know yet. I was intent on being there for her one hundred percent, and I wanted no part in dividing my loyalties.

Simply stated, her life meant more, and it wasn't even close. We were one flesh that could only be divided by death. Self-preservation is one of the most basic of instincts. I believed with my whole heart that God was on our side in this battle for the rest of our lives together and that He had promised *me* that He would deliver me out of darkness.

As I sat by my wife's bedside, hour after hour, throughout the agonizing nights, I was tormented like a convicted felon on death row facing impending doom. It was a vicious cycle of feeling anxious, restless, and discouraged. In fact, I think I felt every negative emotion that there is, and my soul was slowly sinking down.

But I never *begged* God to spare her— not even once. Undoubtedly, begging is beneath me as a child of God, and He doesn't respond generally to our faithless cries of hopelessness. They sound too much like the temper tantrum of a toddler who has outgrown the bottle but is demanding to have it back. Such cries are completely devoid of humility or honor. In the end, God is not moved by our carnal needs as much as He is by our unwavering faith.

Accordingly, I continuously reminded Him of what the Bible says about Him being a way maker and a healer to those who love Him and who are His covenant children. Truthfully, although I was at times completely gripped with fear as I had never known at the very thought of possibly losing Carla, I was also somehow well able to almost immediately beat that evil force back, like a bad habit. Sometimes we have to prophesy to ourselves.

———•●•———

It was always so cold in Carla's room, which I was told was intentional as they were trying to keep her cooler in order to minimize potential brain damage and to maximize recovery. But the room temperature was just another hazard for me to deal with. Sleeping on the floor next to her bed was actually more comfortable than sleeping in the chair. I was experiencing some left hip pain in addition to problems with the lower back and left knee.

I was taking aspirin every four hours or so, and they seemed to help a little. They gave me some extra blankets. I was probably sleep deprived because even though I was getting 8 to 10 hours of sleep every day in my bed, I was restless, and I wasn't able to sleep soundly.

I knew that I looked terrible, so I decided that the easy answer was to simply avoid looking at myself in the mirror. The only reason that I shaved was that I hated the feel of stubble on my face. Other than that, I showered every day and put on clean underwear and socks. My hair generally grew fast, and I needed a haircut badly. But I seriously doubted that soldiers on the battlefield of a great war cared that much about their appearance.

I was meditating with my eyes closed when someone walked into the room.

"Sam," Pastor Justin softly interrupted my inner monologue.

"What are you doing here?" I asked.

"I wanted to check in on Carla. How's she doing?"

I shrugged my shoulders.

"Did somebody call you?" I wondered.

"No, nobody."

"Good."

"I brought you some coffee," he said. "Let's go to the waiting room."

I got up and followed him down the hall. The lights in the waiting room were off, and Pastor turned the light switch on. We sat down next to each other, and he handed me a small white bag. I opened it and took out the large paper cup. I immediately took a sip, and the soothing warmth in my mouth and throat stirred my senses.

"So, how are you doing, Sam?"

"Oh, I could be better."

"So, no sign of improvement?"

"No, not really. What time is it?"

"A little after midnight."

"Oh."

"What does the doctor say?" Pastor solicited.

"Nothing," I replied. "Just that we have to wait and see. The longer she's like this, I guess the worse it is, though."

"How are the babies?"

"Good, as far as I know."

"As far as you know?"

"Uh huh."

"Why haven't you visited them?"

"Because I can't."

"Why not?"

"Because it feels like I'm moving on without Carla," I explained. " And that's something that I simply refuse to do. No, I can wait. There's nothing that I can do for them anyway."

"I'm not so sure about that," he challenged.

"I am," I insisted.

"I see…Don't you think that Carla would understand if you just checked on them every once in a while?"

"Maybe, but it's not up to her," I contended.

"Right."

"Look, I'm not asking anyone to agree with what I'm doing," I offered. "I just know what I need to do for me to give my best effort here."

"It's been a week," Pastor emphasized.

"I know how long it's been."

"I just think that you should pace yourself better," he suggested. "It's clearly not a sprint."

"Yeah, I know."

"How about this, Sam?" he proposed. "You go home now and take care of yourself. I'll stay with Carla the rest of the night until your mother-in-law gets here in the morning. I won't leave her. I promise."

"Uh… thanks… but no… I can't ask you to do that."

"You're not asking," I replied. "I'm offering. Besides, I just want to spend some real time praying over her as her pastor. Please, I want to do it."

"Well…"

"C'mon, Sam," he urged. "Please let me do this for you. I really want to"

"Um… okay. If you're sure."

"I am," he declared. "Thank you, Sam. It's my honor to serve you both."

I was exhausted, and I had to really focus on the short drive home. My eyes were crossing and were heavy. Although there was no real traffic at that time of night, I didn't want to hit anything. That's the last thing I needed.

Carla's car was parked in the driveway in front of her mother's car. I parked next to Carla, walked in through the garage door, and was headed toward the inside door. Out of the corner of my eye, I noticed the large cardboard box in the corner where I had put it almost a month ago. I had forgotten all about it.

The garage was a mess, like every other thing in my life. I had been meaning to organize it, but I never really found the time. It took me a minute to find the box cutter, and I cut the top of the box open and carried it into the house. I placed it on the kitchen table and reached inside and pulled out two stuffed teddy bears. One was dressed in blue overalls, and the other wore a pink and white polka dot dress with a big pink bow in her hair. The outfits were hand-stitched, and the detail was incredible. Their eyes were big and bright.

There was no card in the box, just a note from the manufacturer.

We can't wait to meet you, Mommy and Daddy!
We're here for you to love!

It hit me like a blow to the gut, and I began to sob uncontrollably. The tears poured out like rain from a downburst, the force of which caused me to bend over at the waist. This was actually the first time that I had cried since Carla gave birth. I had been holding it in all of this time, but once it was loosed, like with a broken levee system, there was nothing for me to do but just go with it. My nose was running too, like crazy, and I started coughing and wheezing as I tried to catch my breath. I was just glad that no one was around to see me in such a state.

When I rose up, I hugged both bears as tightly as I could for several minutes. I felt foolish doing it, but at the same time, it was quite soothing too. Thereafter, I carried them upstairs and placed each one gently in the cribs. I then walked to the master bedroom, kicked off my shoes, and got into bed with all my clothes on. I fell asleep almost immediately and slept soundly throughout the rest of the night.

Chapter 15

I hadn't really thought about work at all in almost a week, which was a record for me. But I woke up early and decided to go to the office and check on the status of everything. Nobody was there when I arrived. I was still going through my mail when Tony walked in.

"Hey Sam, I didn't expect to see you here today."

"I just wanted to go through my mail."

"There's nothing there that can't wait." Tony reprimanded. "You didn't have to come in just for the mail. You should have called instead."

"I know, but I also needed a change of scenery. The four walls of Carla's hospital room were starting to close in on me."

"I can only imagine," he replied. "So, how's it going with your wife?"

"She's stable, but she still hasn't woken up yet," I advised.

"Oh, I'm sorry."

"So, what's going on here?" I wondered.

"Um, not a lot, really… But there is one thing that I should probably tell you about."

"What's that?"

"Zoe Carter."

"What about her?"

"Apparently, she got herself all sloshed and drove off the road and hit a house," he related.

"A house? Really?"

"Fortunately, no one got hurt," he said. "She was arrested and was in jail for a day before her parents could bail her out."

"Who is representing her?"

"You are."

"Who?"

"You."

"But…"

"They wanted you," he explained. "I told them that you had a family emergency and weren't available."

"Who handled the arraignment?"

"I did," his eyebrows rose.

"Who?"

"Me."

"You?" I repeated in disbelief.

"Hey, I went to law school too," he said and stuck out his chest.

"I'm sorry…I know… I know you did," I said and chuckled to myself.

"I was terrified," he admitted and shook his head. "I have no idea how you do that stuff."

"It's not really that hard," I answered. "You apparently made it through."

"Barely, but it's all yours now."

"Okay, I got it," I replied. "How's Zoe?"

"A lost soul, I'd say," he remarked and lowered his eyes.

He looked troubled.

"Yeah, I know she is," I acknowledged.

"Do you think that the DWI will impact her civil case?"

"Possibly, but we can always spin it in our favor," I asserted.

"Spin it how?"

"By arguing that the reason why she is drinking so much is that she was sexually harassed by her boss. I'm not sure that's entirely the case, but the harassment definitely didn't help her cause."

"I thought you said he wasn't her boss?" Tony questioned.

"But the insurance company is still responsible for his actions just the same," I explained. "It doesn't matter what his title is. They employed him and were responsible for his actions."

"All right, I gladly leave it in your capable hands."

"Thanks."

"But you don't have to do anything with it now," he stressed. "They aren't going to indict her right now or anything. I say you get out of here and go take care of your wife."

"In a minute. I just have to do a couple of things."

"Let us know if there is anything that we can do," he kindly offered. "We're all thinking good thoughts."

"Thank you. I really appreciate everything."

"No problem."

I was saddened to hear about Zoe, but I really wasn't that surprised. She was clearly crying out for help. She could have killed herself and other innocent people. Pain of the soul is the worst kind of pain that there is. That's the reason that we all— deep down inside— yearn for a savior.

———•●•———

I got a haircut, and then I went back home and did my laundry. There was a lot of food in the refrigerator that people had brought over. I threw out the really old stuff. I also cleaned the bathrooms and went through the mail.

I was on a roll, and what I liked most was that everything that I was doing was mindless. It was the mental break that I needed from fighting to control my thoughts and keep the bad ones at bay. Surprisingly, I wasn't in any hurry to rush back to the hospital, even though I felt a nagging draw to get there. I just needed a second to catch my breath.

Mr. Jenkins was alone in the waiting room when I got there. He was seated with his head back and his eyes closed. Anxiety swirled around him.

"You look better," he said as soon as he gazed upon me. "Pretty."

"Funny. How are things here?"

"Jackie and Christina are with Carla now."

"How are you?" I asked.

"Who knows?"

"She's gonna make it, you know," I whispered.

"How can you be so sure?"

"Just a feeling."

"And you trust it?" he questioned. "This feeling?"

"I do."

"What if you're wrong?"

"I try not to go there," I replied. "I will cross that bridge when I get there. I just know that I will trust God with my dying breath."

"Hmm," he reacted. "You know, I have never had much use for religion. I'm a man of science…I thought my brother was out of his mind when he dropped out of college to become a pastor... I always thought that it was all just a bunch of mumbo jumbo- you know, weak-minded, lazy people who need an escape from their miserable lives."

"A lot of people feel that way," I offered.

"But not you," he invoked.

"No, not me."

"I wish I had that."

"Why?" I wondered aloud. "I mean, if it's all fake."

"Um… because … I guess I've been wondering lately that if I were a… better man, you know, maybe… maybe none of this would be happening to Carla. I feel …exposed. Maybe God is mad at me."

He did a quick laugh and then stopped abruptly.

"I don't think God is mad at you," I refuted. "He's not like that."

"See, you talk about God with such assurance," he stated. "It makes me wonder."

"I don't know everything," I felt impressed to say. "In fact, I'm finding that the more I live, the less I know."

"You're a young man," he pointed out. "It just seems like that. I think you're doing pretty good myself."

"Thank you."

"But I do know that God is real and that He loves us," I insisted.

"Hmm..."

"We can know at least that much," I said.

"I want that assurance," he articulated. "I feel like it's getting harder and harder to breathe. Something has gotta give."

"Tell me about it," I remarked.

"I'm afraid that I'm not going to survive if something bad happens here. I don't have much left."

"Maybe you should talk to Pastor Jenkins," I suggested. "He really helped me before."

"I know…maybe," he answered. "But it hasn't always been easy between us. Our father was a hard man. Our relationship was a casualty of his need to control us in order to impress people."

"If you know that to be the case, then why haven't you done something to make things better?"

"That's what Jackie says too," he offered. "But she can't possibly understand. Things have been *said* between us… you know… Things that are hard to walk back."

"He probably feels the same way, too," I urged. "He's a part of you, and you know it. Maybe you just tell him that."

His breath shook, and he rubbed his forehead with his right hand.

"Who knows?" I posed. "This may be your last chance. You never know."

His face dropped.

———— •●• ————

I waited until I was alone with Carla to go through the closet in her hospital room. This was the first time that I opened that door. I was looking for the notebook with the baby names in it. I found it and quickly shut the door. I was starting to get emotional going through her things.

There were about 30 names listed there, in no particular order. Some names were crossed out, and others were starred. There were lines everywhere connecting two names, and sometimes three. The whole thing looked like some kind of crazy word puzzle. I couldn't help but smile to myself. I loved the way her mind worked.

I studied the names throughout the night. I had to put the notebook down several times because it was all so overwhelming. Some names I could easily delete. Others I really liked, but I didn't like the matching name. I was careful not to write anything in the notebook because I thought it would be a great keepsake for the babies when they grow up.

Carla clearly thought that the babies were both girls, because there was a surplus of girl names. She never told me she thought that. I was secretly hoping that at least one was a boy. In hindsight, it may have been a mistake to opt not to know the sex of the babies beforehand.

I knew that I was making it a lot more complicated than it needed to be. But the choice of a name has lifelong implications that ought not to be ignored or downplayed. They had to be right. I could feel the level of my anxiety rising some more.

But the truth is that Carla would have been worse. Let's just say that decision-making was not her strength. She often agonized over what she should have for dinner. I have no idea how she would have ever even picked one name, let alone two.

I told myself to just trust my gut, and still I kept going

back and forth. Choosing the babies' middle names presented additional hurdles. However, before I drifted off to another restless sleep on the floor, I somehow managed to narrow it down to two sets of names. And when I woke up, I knew, without a doubt, the names of our children — somehow I just knew.

———•●•———

"Hi, Sam."

"Paul, thanks for taking my call. I know how busy you are."

"I'm never too busy for you," he said. "How's private practice treating you?"

"Good," I answered. "I have no complaints now that I don't have to deal with you guys in the district attorney's office every day."

"I think you just miss us," he teased. "What can I do you for?"

"The better question, Paul, is, what can I do for you?"

"Uh oh, sounds like I'm about to get sweet-talked. Aren't you at least going to buy me a drink first?"

"I resent that," I joked.

"You're a big boy," he replied. "I'm sure you'll get over it."

"Zoe Carter," I said. "Maggie just told me that it's your case."

"Who?" he wondered aloud. "Zoe Carter? Not ringing a bell."

"It's a DWI."

"Oh yeah, sorry," Paul said. "She hit a house on Jones

Hill. Her blood level was something crazy high."

"Yes, that's right," I acknowledged. "I know it's early, but she has no priors, and I was just wondering if there is anything that we can do to fast-track this?"

"I can't really reduce the charge because of the accident," he indicated. "Get her some inpatient treatment. There can be no disposition in a case like this that doesn't involve alcohol treatment."

"I figured as much," I conceded. "We are gonna need some time to find the right place."

"Okay, you let me know when you do, and we can talk."
"Will do. Thanks."

— • ● • —

"Pastor Justin, it's me, Sam."
"Hi, Sam, is everything okay?"
"Yes, I'm just calling to thank you again for what you did the other night. It was a blessing!"
"Good, glad to do it. Any change?"
"No, sleeping beauty is still asleep," I replied.
Well, we can't hurry God," he said. "Now can we?"
"No, I guess not."
"But I'm in a better headspace," I articulated. "I just wanted you to know."
"That's an answer to prayers, too," he commented. "So, how are you, Pastor?"
"Me, oh, I'm good."
"…You know, I pray, too."
"What do you mean?"
"I'm just saying that you don't have to talk if you don't

want to, but I know that things have been a little unsettling for you too lately."

"Sam, I don't really think this is the time. Do you?'

"Giving and receiving have to work both ways, kinda like a mutual exchange," I submitted. "Otherwise, it's just charity and not a true friendship."

"That's probably true," Pastor conceded.

"It is true," I contended. "I'm starting to think that sometimes we hear better from God for other people than we do for ourselves."

"I appreciate that, but I want you to focus on your family now," Pastor spoke. "Not on me."

"Okay, just please don't do anything without talking to me first," I insisted. "You know what I'm talking about?"

"…Yes, I think I do…"

"All right."

"Thanks, Sam."

------------•●•------------

I was bum-rushed by Carla's family, who abruptly stopped talking as soon as I walked into the waiting room. Initially, I wasn't sure what to think, and I staggered slightly. But I saw and felt their excitement. It blessed me.

Mrs. Jenkins threw both of her arms around my neck and kissed me hard on the side of my face. Her husband started patting me on the back.

"When did you do that?" Christina asked. "When we went up to check on the babies this morning and saw their names written there, we were in shock!"

"I almost passed out," Mrs. Jenkins related. "I couldn't

stop shaking. I think their names are perfect!"

"How did you decide?" Christina wondered.

"Carla had a list," I answered. "It's all her."

"Honey, we are just so honored," Mrs. Jenkins said and teared up. "We never expected anything like this. I don't know what to say. Thank you!"

"You don't have to thank me."

"So, wait, did you see them?" Christina asked.

"No, I didn't," I answered and winced.

"Do you want to maybe go now?" Carla's mother pleaded and leaned into me. "We can all go up now. They are so beautiful! Might make you feel better."

"…I'm sorry, I can't," I whispered.

"Are you sure, Sam?" Mr. Jenkins asked.

"Yeah, I'm sure," I forced myself to say and tensed up.

"It's okay," he assured with a half-smile. "We got you covered, man."

An awkward uneasiness fell on us all. I was suddenly very uncomfortable in my own skin, and I desperately wanted the moment to pass. I'm pretty sure that my in-laws felt the same way, too.

Mrs. Jenkins hugged me again. I could feel her trembling against me.

I knew how it looked. Most expectant fathers can hardly wait to see their newborn. Typically, holding their baby in their arms for the first time is one of life's most cherished moments. Under most circumstances, I would have been one of them. But once again, things were different for me— something that I definitely had come to expect.

Realistically, however, I knew that I probably had what amounted to the rest of my life to love my children—

hopefully. And believe me, I intended to love them with everything that was within me. They were literally the outward physical manifestation of the miracle that was Carla and me.

More than anything, I wanted them to have all the support that I didn't have when I was growing up. I always hated not having a father, which became my biggest obstacle in life— more than being born Black. I promised myself that I'd never let that happen to my children as long as there was breath in my lungs.

However, much like the good shepherd in the Bible, who left his entire flock to seek and save the one missing sheep that went astray, I felt that I needed to contend for the one under my watch who was most in need and who might possibly slip away for good. Perfect love isn't always logical. But it is steadfast.

To me, that meant following my heart and soul and warring with Carla against the spirit of darkness until she was back with us in every way. I didn't expect anyone to understand. Honestly, I didn't see how they could.

Chapter 16

The screaming phone woke me out of a deep sleep, and I instinctively reached for it. The clock on the nightstand read 10:58 a.m. I had been at the hospital all night, and I had just gotten home. I had only been asleep for about an hour.

"Mr. Hicks, this is Melanie at the ICU at St. Luke's. It looks like your wife is waking up. I wanted to let you know."

In response, I threw my body into motion. I was unable to think— my mind gave over completely to my emotions and to the adrenaline rushing through me. It felt like I had somehow stepped outside of my body, and I was watching at a distance while an unknown force took over and was ordering my steps. I remember distinctly running through the hospital parking lot and standing in the elevator out of breath.

They wouldn't let me on the unit and told me that I needed to go to the waiting room. When I got there, the room was dark and empty. The only sign of life was a small, wilting cactus plant on the windowsill. For some reason, I never noticed it before.

I wondered where Carla's mom was. She was at the

hospital when I left earlier. My whole body was on high alert, and I felt the sweat dripping down my back underneath my shirt. I was unable to sit still.

"Sam."

"What's going on?" I demanded. "Do you know?"

"I was sitting next to the bed, and Carla opened her eyes," Mrs. Jenkins explained. "Just like that. I mean, it came out of nowhere. I'm just so glad that I was there."

"Did she say anything?"

"No, she just opened her eyes, and I ran and got the nurse. Then they all rushed in and told me that I had to leave. The nurse said that she was going to call you, and I just went to call Chris and Christina."

"How long ago was that?"

"I don't know…less than an hour."

"They won't let me in either," I complained.

"I guess we just have to sit here," she concluded. "I don't think Carla recognized me."

"It's still a good sign," I presented.

"I know it is," she replied and put her hand on my thigh for me to stop shaking my leg.

Our eyes met, and I nodded my head. She countered with a reassuring smile and looked away.

Eventually, a doctor, whom I had never seen before, walked into the room. He was tall, thin, with bushy eyebrows, and wore a dark goatee. He tugged at his shirt collar.

"Well, I have some good news, folks," he announced. "It appears that Carla is coming around."

"She's awake?"

"Not fully," he related. "But we have every reason to

believe that she will. Her eyes are responding, even though there are still no motor responses. We expect to see now more localized responses as she slowly begins to awaken."

"Like what?" I questioned.

"Responding to sound, touch, or following movement."

"Can she hear anything now?" I followed up.

"Possibly."

"How long will that take?" Mrs. Jenkins asked.

"Hard to say," the doctor said. "Every patient is different. But this is what we've been waiting for. The longer she remained unconscious, the less likelihood there is of a full recovery."

"So, you think now that she will make a full recovery?" I urged.

"Unfortunately, there is no way to predict what will happen," he replied.

"But you expect her to wake up, right? I mean, she's no longer critical?"

"It's not like you have probably seen in movies or on television where the patient just suddenly wakes up fully," he explained. "People don't usually just open their eyes and get up and climb out of bed. It's a process."

I sulked. As I was running across the parking lot, I had visions of Carla sitting up in bed, looking beautiful and anxiously waiting for me to get there. This was a bit of a bummer. I was obviously getting ahead of myself.

"But it's important to remember that this is the first real step toward recovery that we have seen since she gave birth," the doctor reinforced. "There is reason to be encouraged."

"Can we see her now?" Mrs. Jenkins asked.

"In a minute. We are almost done."

"Okay, thanks," she expressed and sighed heavily.

"Yeah…thanks," I muttered.

"Anything else I can tell you?" he asked.

I shook my head.

"No, I think we're good."

"By the way, my name is Dr. Donohue. I don't think that we met before. Please let me know if there is anything that I can do."

"Nice to meet you."

"Likewise," he said. "I'll tell them to come get you when they're done."

As soon as he walked away, I realized that I had another throbbing headache. I was just overtired and running on fumes. But I was getting very good at ignoring my body. My personal needs remained secondary.

Carla looked the same to me. She had her eyes closed and appeared to be sleeping. They had changed and removed some of the tubes and things, so it looked less cluttered, but nothing else in the room had changed. It still felt cold and impersonal.

"Carla?" I whispered. "Carla? Can you hear me? Wake up, sleepyhead! Are you ready to get up and go home? The babies are here. They can't wait to meet their mom. I'm so proud of you…It's gonna be great, all of us together at last. Just the way we planned. I think that you will be the best mother in the whole world. I can hardly wait."

I looked at her mother, who walked up to her daughter's bedside and leaned in and kissed her on the forehead.

"Carla, it's Mom," she whispered and inched forward. "I love you, baby… Let me know when you are ready to get up. I'll finish helping you get the house ready… You're going to have your hands full with these twins. I have seen them, and they are magnificent, I tell you… So beautiful and perfect and *waiting for you to love*… Wait until you see them. We all love them so much already… All they need now is their momma."

Mrs. Jenkins fought back tears. We hovered there for several minutes, sprinkling our love down upon her like a springtime mist. Suddenly, Carla's eyes fluttered and her face contorted. It lasted only a couple of seconds, but we both saw it clearly and hovered closer.

"Carla, honey?" her mother begged. "Carla?"

Nothing really happened after that, although we both froze in place and anxiously waited for more. Several minutes of stifling silence filled the room. We eventually exhaled and stepped back. Still, my spirit soared because I could finally see with my physical eyes that God was working out the miracle that I was expecting all along.

Mrs. Jenkins told me that I was snoring, and that I needed to go home and get some sleep. I sat straight up in the chair and started considering my options. It was 1:30 p.m. Although I really didn't want to leave, I reluctantly agreed to go. The roller-coaster-like spikes in emotions were weighing heavily on me. My body ached, especially my left leg, and my headache had only gotten worse.

I took a hot shower as soon as I got home. I mistakenly thought it would relax me before I jumped into bed. But instead, it had the opposite effect on me. My brain was on overload, and I couldn't turn it off enough to go to sleep. It felt like I was back in law school, and I was cramming for a test that I had to take the next day.

However, at least back then, I knew that the pain would

soon be over, and I would be able to go on the same as before, like nothing ever happened. That was essentially the way it was for every test that I had ever taken and passed in my life. It was true for the bar exam. It was also true for getting past all of the dysfunction in my youth.

Indeed, I was programmed for most of my life to just close my eyes tight, shelter in place, and endure until the storm was over. Although there are scriptures that seem to teach that all we needed to do was wait upon the Lord and that everything will be okay, not every test is the same, because there would be no real growth if that were the case. Seasons change, and some tests are easier to get through than others.

It felt different now, and I was more than a little lost— and scared. Somehow, things had completely shifted both in me and around me. Suddenly, the uphill road upon which I had been traveling since I was born was getting even more rocked— not less. The stakes were higher than ever before, and my sense was that I needed to do more than just cower and hide like a victim— something that I definitely wasn't.

The truth is that there was no telling how much longer Carla was going to be down. She had been completely weaned off the sedatives used to sedate her for a while and was just beginning to show signs of regaining consciousness. Some battles last a long time— even a lifetime. The highest goal ought to be not just to learn to withstand the pain and setbacks in life but rather to use them to become more Christlike and to live victoriously as a testimony that our God reigns.

Regardless of what happens with Carla and the babies, things were definitely going to be very different for me spiritually going forward. The die had already been cast and, according to my spirit, I needed to face it head-on, or risk failing this critical test. I heard that quiet direction clearly within me. and it sent me reeling. That's the real reason why I couldn't sleep.

Chapter 17

And just like that, Carla woke up. She couldn't talk, but she gradually became more alert over a 48-hour period and recognized us. She had some right-side paralysis and muscle weakness. She also had no recollection of being induced or giving birth. She barely remembered being pregnant. The doctor said that she would need both speech and physical therapy, but the overall prognosis was good. Needless to say, we were overjoyed.

She kept crying, which literally broke my heart. She used to complain that I acted like I could feel her every feeling, but I did think that we were more connected than most couples. I tried to reassure her that everything was going to be okay, but she wasn't hearing it. Understandably, she woke up in a bad mood.

Everyone wanted to see Carla, and they were all doing everything they could to tend to her every need. Unfortunately, however, she wasn't really cooperating. I could see both sides of it. They were all just so happy to have her back and needed to shower her with love and affection. At the same time, she wasn't aware of everything that we had all been through in the past week and a half, and she was ornery and in pain. We all had been through hell, and none of us were at our best.

Moreover, she was never a good patient before, and her family knew that about her. She was strong-willed and stubborn, no doubt about it. However, they were very much taken aback at the way she was acting. I could see the hurt on their faces.

Carla always told me that her family was just as dysfunctional as mine, that they just hid it better. But I never really saw it until now. A part of me wished that they would all give us a little time alone to regroup, but I knew that that was probably asking too much.

Nothing satisfied her. Understandably, she wanted to see the babies more than anything, but the nurse said that she needed to get stronger before she could be taken to the NICU. Her eyes flooded with tears, and her body shook.

"I promise that we will go up as soon as you feel better," I said.

She burned with rage, and she clenched her left fist.

"No." I quickly reprimanded. "Don't even try that. You know you are still weak and sore. I haven't seen them yet either. I wanted to wait for you. It won't be long now. We'll go up together."

She gave me a dismissive wave of her left hand.

"I was out of my mind when I thought that I might lose you," I articulated. "I'm not going to take any chances now by rushing things. You are gonna have to trust me."

I could see the disappointment in her eyes. I leaned over and kissed the side of her face. Her gaze met mine briefly, and she relaxed a little.

"Is there anything else that you need- something I can

get you, maybe?"

She shook her head no.

"I love you, you know," I whispered. "…Do you still love me because you haven't really said?"

She gradually raised her head like a shy kid being called on in class by the teacher. Her eyes sparked.

"I still don't understand why I always have to be the first one to say it," I teased.

———•●•———

We met our children nine days after Carla woke up. They were intubated and ventilated in two separate crib-type enclosures. They appeared to also be in some kind of plastic bags, and one wore a blue knitted hat, and the other wore a pink one. They were so small that they could probably fit into the palm of my hand. It was hard to see their faces or their eyes clearly. I thought their skin color was slightly off.

Carla gasped loudly with her first look at them through the viewing window. A raw wave of emotion hit us both at the same time. For me, there was an overriding sense of awe and wonder, and I felt unadulterated love rise up inside of me like never before. Time stood still.

"Oh!" Carla somehow managed to get out, and she covered her mouth with her left hand. Her breaths quickened.

The nurse holding Carla's wheelchair patted her on the shoulder in comfort and support.

I couldn't believe my eyes and instinctively held my breath. For some reason, they didn't look anything like I had envisioned. Mrs. Jenkins told me that they were tiny, but they looked more frail and endangered than I had imagined. For some reason, I had been thinking that they were more developed, like the babies I saw in church on Sundays. They barely looked real to me.

Sweat beaded my forehead, and I was unsteady on my feet. In my head, I heard only the sound of the ocean, like in a seashell. My thoughts were quieted, and my heart paralyzed. I think that I could have stood there forever gazing at them.

I only saw slight movement in them both. We stood there for several minutes taking it all in. I waved to them as if I was trying to get their attention. We didn't say anything to each other.

"I have to get you back," the nurse said softly. Her soft eyes were reassuring, and we both complied without objection. I gently squeezed her hand as we were turned away. We both looked longingly back at our future as we were being taken away.

"You okay?" I asked as soon as she was back in her bed and the nurse had left the room.

"No," she uttered in a faint voice that still didn't sound anything like her.

"What's wrong? The babies are doing good. They're just small and need time for their lungs to develop."

"I...I..."

She reached for the writing pad next to the bed and wrote:

I don't remember them.

"What do you mean?" I questioned. "You mean you don't remember the delivery?"

Her eyes were wet, and her shoulders slumped. She

looked wounded.

I knew how she felt because there was a big part of me that felt the same way. We were denied the opportunity to truly experience the highs that come from seeing your children being born and holding them. It's hard to ignore that. Sometimes, it seemed that I didn't know God at all or anything about Him.

"I told you that you had a C-section, and they had to put you to sleep," I contended. "That's not your fault. You didn't do anything wrong. It just happens that way sometimes. But they are still a gift from God, and we can love them now as much as we want to ... forever and ever! Okay?"

She sniffled and faked a smile.

"It's gonna all work out." I encouraged further. "You'll see."

Her expression softened.

"...Uh...names?" she asked clearly.

"Oh, sorry. Their names are *Sampson Christopher* and *Carly Jacqeline*."

I could see her thinking... Slowly, her mouth twisted... and then her whole countenance lit up. She displayed the cutest lopsided grin- so cute!

"Ah, see, you like it, don't you?" I taunted. "You should because I read your mind."

It turns out that seeing the twins was the best of all medicines for Carla. She was a little more stable after our visit with them. Since awakening, it had been hard to get her to be fully present. She kept saying that she was tired, but she actually seemed to be a little depressed, which her doctor said was normal.

However, she also wasn't really engaging with her

therapists either. While it didn't appear that she had any cognitive or mental impairment, she was going to have to work to get her body back in shape, and so far, she hadn't shown any real interest in doing that. I was already starting to wonder how she was ever going to be able to take care of two babies at home by herself all day. But we still had some time as the babies only had moderate weight gain since birth, and they were nowhere near the -five-pound benchmark needed to be discharged and sent home.

Carla was moved from intensive care and into a room with another woman, which meant that I had stopped sleeping in her room at night. Her right-side paralysis affected her face, tongue, arm, and leg. She seemed to be making some small gains, and she could walk with assistance. She visited the twins several times a day and was receiving visits from more people. I was starting to see sparks of her old self.

However, her mood continued to fluctuate, and she could be snappy. Her voice was raspy, and her speech was garbled, but I could understand her. I thought she sounded adorable, and I joked about wanting to turn off the lights and for her to whisper sweet nothings in my ear. She was only slightly amused.

"Sam, something is wrong with you," she admonished.

"Why? It's just the truth. I can prove it to you if you want."

"No, thank you," she shot down.

"You are hurting my feelings."

"Sam, stop playing around," she said and yawned. "You're acting crazy!"

"No, I'm not."

"Oh, did you do this?" she asked and pulled the sheets back to reveal her feet.

"What?'

"Did you paint my toes this red color?" she demanded.

"What?" I asked and cringed.

"Did you do this to my toes?"

"Um… I don't know... maybe... why?" I stammered. "What difference does it make?"

She giggled… for the first time in a long time, and I melted for a second.

"When did you do it?" she pressed.

"Never mind," I replied and looked away from her.

"I can't believe you *painted my toenails!*" she articulated clearly.

She giggled some more. I was very embarrassed. I scolded myself for letting myself get so carried away.

"So, what's the problem?" I rose up. "Just let it go. It's nothing."

"Mm-hmm, I know," she reassured. "I think it's sweet."

She touched her hand to her heart.

"You already know … you make me crazy," I griped and drew in a long breath. "Just let me *adore* you all right, and leave me alone."

Chapter 18

Zoe Carter was scheduled to complete 30 days of inpatient treatment at an alcohol treatment facility. She agreed to go under protest and held fast to her claim that she didn't have a drinking problem despite the fact that her blood alcohol level when she was arrested was more than twice the legal limit. Most people wouldn't have been able to function at all under those circumstances and would have passed out somewhere with that much alcohol in their system.

She wanted to argue about it, but I refused to go there with her. Rather, I simply presented her with her two choices. That is, either she went to rehab, or she spent some more quality time in the women's unit in the county jail. She clearly wasn't happy with either option.

Their family dysfunction was now on full display before me. I received two separate phone calls from Zoe's parents, where they essentially blamed each other for everything that was wrong with her. They both used colorful language, which I didn't appreciate and chose to ignore. I understood that they both loved their daughter in their own separate ways and were mostly just venting.

Contrary to my initial impression, Zoe's mother was the

controlling personality in the marriage. From her own mouth, she was disrespectful to her husband and carried some unspoken grievances against him. In her mind, he wasn't fully committed to their family and wasn't a good father. She didn't trust or respect his judgment.

"I had to do everything," she complained. "Every time I tried to set boundaries with Zoe, he gave in to her behind my back. He spoiled her. That's why she's not grounded at all, and she's all over the place."

In response, Joe claimed that his wife was self-centered and refused to listen to anyone. She apparently used to punish Zoe all the time for minor infractions when she was young and was overbearing. He felt that she didn't really know how to show or receive affection.

Moreover, his wife allegedly regularly bad-mouthed him to Zoe, which he found to be a major breach of decorum.

"She's not a happy person, and she goes out of her way to make everyone else around her miserable, too," he declared. "So, I basically leave her alone, which is really what she wants anyway."

"If things are so bad, why didn't you just leave?" I questioned.

"Because I don't believe in divorce," he maintained. "My first marriage was annulled by the church. Believe you me, that took a lot of doing to accomplish. I've had my one bite at the apple. So, I'd say that I'm pretty much screwed."

I had no desire to be a family counselor, and listening to them was very uncomfortable for me. While understanding how Zoe got in this predicament in the first place could be an important part of helping her, this was all too much information for me. Ultimately, Zoe was a grown woman, and I was just her lawyer— not her counselor or her savior.

I insisted upon meeting with Zoe alone, without her parents. She was going to an alcohol facility in Florida in less than a week. She mostly just listened as I explained to her that the primary goal had to be to make sure that she didn't end up with a criminal record, something that could stay with her for the rest of her life.

"That means that you have to do everything you can to get this conviction expunged from your record," I appealed.

"When will I get my driver's license back?" she asked.

"That will be up to the judge and the DMV. We can deal with that later."

"I didn't hurt anybody," she argued. "I mean…nobody died or anything. "

"But a car in the hands of a drunk driver is a weapon," I lectured. "Somebody could have died. You were lucky."

She sighed, and sat back, and crossed her arms in front of her.

"I'm not an alcoholic," she disputed. "I'm not…I'm not like that."

"What is an alcoholic?" I posed.

"Um…I don't really know."

"Then how do you know that you're not physically addicted to alcohol?" I questioned. "That can happen to anyone."

"Because I can stop drinking anytime that I want," she alleged.

"So, you don't want to stop?" I countered. "Zoe, is that what you're telling me? That you don't want to stop? Is that what this is about?"

She refused to answer me. Instead, her cocoa brown eyes turned off as she shifted nervously in her seat and picked at her nails. I understood that to mean that she really wasn't interested in anything else that I had to say.

I felt sorry for her, but the last thing she needed from me was my pity. A drowning person needs a helping hand and a lifeline- not sympathetic onlookers. Hopefully, this expensive program that her mother found for her would do the trick for her. Otherwise, I feared that she was headed for more serious problems in the future.

I quickly worked out a deal with the assistant district attorney that required Zoe to enter a plea to DWI, a misdemeanor, with the promise of no jail time. She was understandably nervous standing next to me in court. She kept fidgeting with her hair and spoke softly. Both of her parents were present. I knew she was embarrassed.

The judge made her state in open court everything she did that night before her arrest, including exactly what she was drinking and how much of it she consumed. Apparently, she really liked cosmopolitans. I never asked her that question beforehand, and I didn't even know what a cosmopolitan was. For some reason, I had just assumed that she was drinking beer. Her sentencing was scheduled to take place in six weeks, after she had completed her rehab program.

———————— • ● • ————————

I went to church for the first time in a month. Everyone was happy to see me, and I received a lot of loving hugs. It felt good to be back. Mama came with me, and I could tell that she had missed being there, too. Our church family had become a source of strength for us.

I was surprised to see Lacey Stanton singing up front with the worship team. I just assumed that she had left the church or at least was keeping a low profile. But there she was pretty much dead center, dancing and singing in front of Pastor Justin. I wondered how Pastor Marlene felt about that.

I didn't get a chance to talk to Pastor Justin afterward. He left the sanctuary as soon as he finished preaching, and three women immediately cornered me and peppered me with questions about Carla and the babies. I figured that I would catch up with him later.

I had to call him twice and leave two messages before he called me back the next day.

"Hi Pastor, I was just checking in with you."

"Uh, thanks," he replied. "I have just been so busy."

"Doing what?"

"We met with some guy about expanding the sanctuary," he offered. "It's going to cost a lot more than we ever imagined."

"Everything costs a lot today," I echoed.

"How's Carla?"

"She coming around, I guess. She doesn't like doing her therapies."

"Can you blame her? She's already been through so much."

"I know."

"I saw you yesterday," Pastor said. "Good to have you back."

"Tell you the truth, I was surprised to see Lacey leading worship," I remarked.

"Really? Why?"

"Because I thought you were distancing ourselves from her."

"I never said that," he objected. "Resurrection is still her church. I'm not going to kick her out."

"Oh, sorry, my mistake." I apologized. "I was thinking that…"

"I'm just not going to meet with her anymore."

"But don't you think you should completely distance yourself?" I questioned. "She's trouble for you."

"How?" he asked sharply.

"Let me put it to you this way, if I were her husband, I would come to service next Sunday, walk up front, and punch you in the face."

"I don't know why you have to always act like we're doing something wrong."

"Well, I don't know," I spoke and hesitated. "Are you doing something wrong?"

"I told you I never touched her," he vented. "You keep going there."

"But she wants you to."

"I can't help that."

"Sure, you can," I insisted. "What does Pastor Marlene think?"

"Why do you keep bringing up Marlene?" he challenged. "I'm sick of hearing that from you."

"Because I suspect that she is seeing things differently from you."

"Our relationship is based upon mutual respect," he purported. "Marlene trusts me."

"But does she trust Lacey?"

"Lacey can't make me do anything that I don't want to do."

"Wanna bet," I refuted. "She already has."

"I have no idea what you are saying."

"You can't ignore your wife's feelings," I asserted.

"I'm doing no such thing."

"So, you're telling me that you want her to be up there singing on Sundays?" I prodded. "You don't have a problem with it?"

"Matter of fact, I don't," he dug in. "It's good for her."

"Apparently, it's good for you, too."

"What's that supposed to mean?"

"I think you know."

"Actually, I don't," he claimed. "You know, I kinda wish that I never told you about any of this."

"Why?"

"Because you can be very judgmental," he alleged. "Not everything is as black and white as you seem to think it is."

"I speak from experience," I debated. "Did you forget what happened to me when I gave a mentally unstable woman the benefit of the doubt. She ended up stabbing me in the side."

"This is different," he asserted.

"Really?" I ridiculed. "How's it different, Pastor? Cause I'm not exactly seeing it?"

"You know it's different!" he insisted. "Lacey isn't *...mentally unstable*. She's just in a bad place. That thing with you and Kiana isn't the same at all."

"You thought Kiana was fine up until the moment she tried to kill me," I doubled down. "You missed it then, and you're missing it now."

"Aw… c'mon!" he exclaimed. "This is not the same situation, and you know it. Kiana was… uh she was…"

"Some crazy *Black* woman?"

"I didn't say that," he protested. "Please don't put words in my mouth."

"Then what is it?"

He was at a loss for words.

"They both want something that they can't have," I clarified. "What's the difference?"

"Are you trying to say that you think that Lacey is going to try to hurt me?"

"I don't know, maybe, if she doesn't get what she wants," I asserted.

"I think that's absurd," he denounced. "They are nothing alike!"

"Why?" I needled. "Because you trust her sunny blue eyes?"

Pastor didn't answer again. But I could hear him quietly raging.

"Look, Pastor, I'm sorry," I said. "But I'm just trying to get you to see…."

"What I *see* is that you are biased against Lacey for some unknown reason."

"That's not true."

"You probably haven't ever spoken one word to her!" he challenged.

"Pastor, I'm just telling you that you are in over your head again with this," I contended. "You're too… *invested* here for some reason."

"Maybe so, but it's *my* problem, not yours," he maintained. "You're in no position to judge anyone."

"What's that supposed to mean?" I pressed.

"What do you think it means?"

"I don't know. Why don't you tell me?"

"Never mind," he said. "I don't want to talk about this anymore."

"If you have something against me, you should just say it," I demanded. "Just be a man about it."

"I'm sorry, but this conversation is over."

"Okay, that's fine with me," I replied. "You're on your own. The two of you can have at it for all I care."

"Works for me," he said. "So enjoyed our little talk."

"You have a good night, Pastor."

I stewed about this interaction for a long while afterward— probably too long. I know that in certain situations, I can be overly frank. It's a family trait that I can't fully harness. But Pastor's comments touched a nerve, and my feelings were hurt because I thought we understood each other better than we obviously did.

To be clear, I really appreciated everything that he had done for me and Carla in the hospital, and otherwise. He had gone out of his way to be there for us— for me. He was more than a pastor; he showed himself to be a true friend to me. I will be forever grateful to him for that.

However, we obviously know people on levels. Perhaps Pastor Justin and I were too different after all, and we weren't really as close as it seemed. I know we care about each other. But two things can be true at the same time, meaning we can love the idea or the dream, but not the reality inside of it.

Indeed, the fact that we were both Christians didn't necessarily mean that we were on the same page in terms of our worldviews, or in the way that we saw each other. Unfortunately, the racial divide in this country is growing, even in the church. True believers today still struggle with the same sins, prejudices, and strongholds as everybody else. We just hide them better most of the time- because we know better.

It appeared that our many differences created too big a gulf between us for us to be anything more than fellow worshipers, with no true meeting of the minds. Honestly, that would be a big blow to me personally because I was hoping for more. Clearly, there are limitations on human relationships because, in the end, we are only completely known and understood by God Himself.

I knew that it was probably a mistake on my part to jump to any concrete conclusions in the wake of one disagreement. Pastor Justin was a good guy, for sure. But people tend to reveal their true heart over time if they are given the opportunity to do so. I couldn't help but wonder if I was the one who was being naïve.

Chapter 19

Carla was discharged from the hospital to finish her therapies at home. Her blood pressure was normal, and her liver function was not impaired. We were warned that there still might be some lingering complications, but these could be minimized with proper care. She was encouraged to resume as many daily activities as she could comfortably tolerate.

At 12 weeks, the twins were not growing at the same pace. Carly was further along than Sampson. He wasn't sucking and swallowing like his sister did and was having some breathing problems. The doctor said that it was too soon to be concerned about it because babies don't grow at the same rate, not even twins. But that was absurd, of course, we were worried – very worried. Leaving the twins at the hospital was really hard. Carla sobbed like a baby herself on the short ride home.

"It'll be all right," I said. "We just have to be patient."

"No, it won't," she cried.

"This is progress for us," I maintained. "They are growing and getting stronger every day. They just need a little more time."

"They need me," she cried.

"And they have you," I emphasized. "We're not going anywhere."

"Is the nursery ready?" she shifted.

"Yes, I already told you. It's all set."

"What if I can't lift them because of my hand?" she obsessed.

"That's why it's important to stay with your physical therapy," I said. "You heard the doctor. They think that you will make a full recovery."

"What if I don't?" she followed up. "You'll be at work all day."

"Your mother has promised to help us. There are other people, too- my grandmother is just dying to get her hands on them. There'll be plenty of help for us."

"Sam, I'm sorry that I let you down," she muttered. "I don't know…"

Her speech was still a little marbled.

"What?" I reacted. "I don't know what you're talking about. You did great. Everybody at the hospital was impressed by how far you have come in such a short time. You're amazing!"

"I think they were just saying that," she resisted.

"You're stronger than you know," I insisted. "I don't know why you never see it. Everybody else does."

"I dreamed I dropped them on the nursery floor, and I couldn't pick them up," she blubbered. "It was so awful!"

"It's just a dream," I replied. "Means nothing. We got this."

"Will you come home for lunch?"

"If you need me to—no problem."

"Thank you," she said, and put her head down and rolled her shoulders.

I reached over and rubbed the top of her thigh. She didn't look up.

We discussed her anxiety and restlessness with Dr. O'Connor. Christina was very opposed to her sister taking an antidepressant— something about side effects. I wasn't sure. I knew that Carla was struggling, and being home presented new problems. Carla said she felt fine, but I knew better. In the end, we decided that she would start taking the antidepressant that her counselor had her taking last year before she was pregnant.

Her mood changed for the better as soon as we walked into the house, and she saw all the people. It was mostly her family. Even her uncle, Pastor Jenkins, was there. Mama was there too. I was reluctant to throw a party, but her mother insisted. She was right.

The living room was full of gifts and flowers from well-wishers. The people from her job sent a pink and white floral bouquet that was truly magnificent. The church sent a fruit basket. Carla was overwhelmed and insisted on reading every card and note right then and there. It was a happy homecoming after all.

•●•

I was feeling pretty beaten up. My body ached, especially my left leg, and I was feeling like I had the weight of the world on my shoulders. I was sleeping, but I was restless, and I woke up still tired. I was glad to be back at work, but I felt guilty that I had missed so much time in the office. This was still a new job for me, and I felt like I hadn't really proven my worth yet.

I hadn't forgotten about the panic attack I had before the twins were born. I finally made an appointment to see my doctor. I only told Carla that I was going in for a routine physical because I didn't want her to worry. But I secretly feared that there might be something seriously wrong with me.

"So, tell me again how long you have been feeling like this?" Dr. Mitchell asked.

He appeared to be in his early 40s with dark brown hair that was just beginning to recede, heavy eyebrows and very thin lips. He wasn't my regular doctor, but he had an opening, and he could see me sooner.

I was sitting on the examination table with my shirt off, and he was standing in front of me. A male nurse was sitting at a small desk in the corner taking notes.

"Uh, I don't know," I replied. "For a couple of months, I'd say. The preeclampsia was tough on us even before all the birth stuff happened. I have been too worried about my wife and the babies to take care of myself. I think that it's all just catching up to me now."

"Sounds like you've been through quite a lot," he sympathized. "My wife just had a baby last year, and I know how hard it was on us. I'm a doctor, and I couldn't believe that anyone thought that it was a good idea to send my son home alone with us. I can't imagine how it's been for you."

"You do what you gotta do, right?" I said.

"Yes, but men suffer physically during the pregnancy too," he contended. "Your blood pressure is actually good today, and your heart sounds good, too. I'm going to order a blood workup on you, though, and I want you to get that done as soon as possible."

"Okay," I replied. "No problem."

"I also think that you might benefit from taking something for your anxiety. Just a small dosage. It should help."

"You want me to take an antianxiety drug?"

"The panic attack you had shouldn't be ignored," the doctor explained. "Your body is trying to tell you something. You probably should have called us right away."

"I don't like drugs."

"It's just temporary," he stated. "But I really think that you need something to help you get through what is a very stressful and trying time in your life. You need your rest and time to recover."

"I know, but..."

"Look, I get it," he interrupted. "We guys have to be there for our families. But we are human too. There is no shame in getting some help."

"My wife is already taking something."

"There you go, the two shall become one," he spoke.

I laughed as I wasn't expecting the Bible reference.

"Well... if you really think so," I relented.

"I do," he replied. "But you can talk to Dr. Abbott about it if you like. I have no problem with that. But to me, it's a no-brainer. The kind of pressure that you have been under can actually weaken your immune system and make you really sick."

"Okay, I hear you... I guess I'll take it."

"Getting some regular physical activity might help you, too." he suggested. "Being behind a desk all day is not doing you any good."

"Okay."

"Please make sure you fast before you go to the lab to get your blood work."

"Okay, I will."

Obviously, I was glad that I went in to see the doctor. I knew that it was foolish to continue to ignore all that I was feeling. Fortunately, the blood work didn't show anything off with me, and I was very grateful and relieved not have to worry about it anymore. Things were slowly starting to look up.

A big part of my problem was that I didn't have anyone whom I could talk to about my problems. I knew that my thinking could be circular at times, which often left me feeling stuck and made me my own worst enemy. I usually liked to talk to Pastor Justin at those times, but that was now absolutely out of the question. I didn't care if I ever spoke to him again.

And I felt that I couldn't really talk to Carla either, who clearly had enough on her plate already. I wanted to protect her from the world more than ever before. Obviously, I wasn't planning to do that forever. For one thing, she wouldn't like it very much if she knew that I was shielding her from the world. She was always bothered if she thought I was being overprotective in the least.

But I also really valued her opinion and had come to rely on her. She was a good sounding board. However, it was fair to assume that she needed a minute to catch her breath before being thrown back into the deep end of things again.

That meant that I was basically alone going into this new chapter in my life. I knew that the heat was going to get turned up a level or two when the twins came home, and that I needed to brace myself for sleepless nights, endless baths, and diaper changes. I was embarrassed to admit even to myself that I had mixed feelings about them being discharged soon.

I reluctantly started taking the anti-anxiety medication that Dr. Mitchell had prescribed for me. But I can't honestly say that it made me feel any different. I still couldn't sleep soundly — even Carla noticed that about me. I figured that, like most soldiers who have been to battle, I just needed a little more time to readjust to life in the real world.

After giving it some thought, it occurred to me that maybe God wanted me to put my trust in Him more and not rely too much on anyone or anything else. After all, He's the one who brought me this far— nobody or nothing else. It's important to keep in the forefront of our minds at all times where our help really comes from.

— • ● • —

I felt guilty. I hadn't seen Hasan, my former client from when I was in the public defender's office, in eight weeks. He was still confined at Marcy Correctional Facility, and although I always liked seeing him, I hated the idea of being inside a prison. There was a heavy, oppressive spirit about the place that always lingered with me long after I left.

Hasan was in the general population now, no longer being held in solitary confinement, where we used to meet. Because I had once represented him, I was still listed as his attorney, and I was able to meet with him alone in a private side room set aside for attorneys meeting with their clients, rather than in the main visitation area used mostly for inmate families.

He had a big grin on his face when he walked into the room and saw me sitting there. That actually made me feel worse because I was aware that I was the only visitor he ever received. My original plan was to try to come and see him at least once a month. But after Carla got sick, I found that there wasn't enough time in my day to keep up that schedule.

He looked good, like the healthy young man that he was. He wore his state-issued green uniform well, which showed off his muscular physique. I was always amazed at how much he had adapted to being locked away from society and seemed to be at peace with everything. I envied him in that small regard.

"Sam, how are you?" he asked as soon as he sat down in the empty seat in front of me.

I could tell that he was genuinely glad to see me, which warmed my heart.

"I'm good," I replied. "It's good to see you."

"You too, man. What's new? How's your wife?"

"Um, she had the twins a month ago," I reported. "That's where I've been. It was tough going there for a while. She had to be induced because she was having so many problems. She almost died. The babies were premature, and they are still in the hospital. We are hoping to bring them home soon."

"That is so great," he said. "I am so happy for you both. What did she have?"

"A boy and a girl. We named them Sampson and Carly."

"Sampson is a strong manly name!" he responded. "I

like it!"

"Thanks."

"Is your wife okay now?"

"She is still recovering."

"I'll be sure to pray for her tonight."

"Thank you."

"Oh, and thank you for the money you put in my account," he said. "I told you before that you didn't have to do that."

"Forget about it," I replied. "My pleasure."

"I appreciate it, man."

"You're very welcome."

"So how does it feel to be a father?"

"I feel overwhelmed already, and I haven't even really held them yet," I related.

"But it's such a blessing!" he declared. "Look at how much God loves you!"

"I know He does."

"So, that's why you look so tired, huh?" he questioned.

"I don't know," I answered. "Frankly, I'm still trying to catch my breath after everything."

"If it were me, I'd be walking around with my chest all stuck out like I was the heavyweight champion of the world. More than anything, I want a family."

"I know," I said. "I really am happy, but it's just that there is a lot that comes with it."

"Can you maybe take some time off work just to be with your family for a while?" he wondered. "You know, they used to do stuff like that in the Bible."

"Not really," I answered. "I've already been out of the office for too long."

"So, what do you want God to do for you in all of this?" he inquired.

"Well…um… that's a good question," I spoke. "I think that I just um want… for everything to settle down for good. I want the babies to get out of danger and come home. And I want Carla to get back to where she was before she got pregnant. She is so accomplished and so beautiful. I feel like she has lost a lot because of me."

"Because of you?" he questioned. "What did you do?"

"Getting married and pregnant has changed the course of her life for the worse."

"Did she say that?"

"She didn't have to."

"My guess is that she doesn't agree with you about that," he stated. "I'm not sure that too many women think like that."

"Maybe not," I conceded.

"And you know that things will eventually settle down."

"Yeah, I know."

"So, what else?" he pressed.

"What makes you think that there is more?"

"Just my sense."

"I got into a fight with my pastor," I said.

"About what?" he asked.

"Nothing really. He has a problem with this woman at the church, and when I questioned him about it, he turned on me."

"Turned on you how?"

"He made it seem like I couldn't possibly understand the situation because it involves a pretty little white woman."

"Did he actually say that?"

"No, he refused to say it," I said. "But he insinuated it."

"Are you sure about that?"

"Pretty sure…maybe."

"Well, he's entitled to his opinion, right?" Hassan pointed out. "He's a grown man."

"Right and normally, I wouldn't care," I stressed. "But I thought we were different."

"Because he is your pastor?" Hasan wondered.

"Because he is my friend…supposedly."

"Even good friends get it wrong sometimes," he suggested.

"Let me ask you this," I said. "Do you think that a white man can really understand a Black man?"

"Understand what exactly?" he questioned and twisted his face.

"You know, the way we are… the way we think."

"I guess it depends."

"On what?"

"On who and what you are talking about," he asserted. "Not all white people are the same any more than all Black people are the same."

"I know that, but we will never be on even ground," I submitted.

"Obviously, most of the guards in here are white," he set forth. "Some of them are cool, but most of them are a problem – and some are straight-up evil. The point is that I will always see them as being different from me— even the good ones. It doesn't mean anything— we can still relate to each other."

"Sure, it does," I contested. "That means that there will always be something between us and them that prevents us from truly seeing each other the way that we really are."

"God's people come from every nation and every tribe," he reflected. "He wants us to get to the point where we love each other the way we love ourselves."

"That's true, but…"

"Loving like that is the goal," he asserted. "It doesn't happen overnight, and it definitely doesn't come easy."

"So, it's always gonna be a thing," I concluded.

"If you must know, I don't understand most Black people myself either, let alone white people," he commented with a bit of a chuckle. We are all different, men from women, the Chinese from the Japanese, whatever, man."

"So, what are you really saying?" I questioned. "That it's a foolish notion to expect that anyone will view you through the right lens?"

"I'm saying love takes time," he expressed. "I'm saying you should probably give your pastor a break because everyone has specks in their eyes, including you. Control what you can control. Do your part in getting to know and understand him."

I didn't say anything.

"Forgiving is a big part of love, too," he continued. "People never talk about that yet, where would we be if God hadn't forgiven us?"

I rubbed my eyes with my thumb and forefinger of my left hand. My brain was still very tired, just apparently not tired enough to rest.

"It'll be okay," he encouraged. "You're trying to get it right. That means that you are teachable. Give yourself a break, too. It sounds like you have been really going through some rough waters."

"Hmm…okay," I reluctantly agreed and nodded my head.

"The way I see it is the only way that we are ever going to get past the racial stuff in this country, and in the world, is to focus on our similarities and not so much on our differences," he opined. "Otherwise, God can't be truly glorified on the earth because together we reflect His glory."

"That's probably true," I conceded.

"That sounds like it should be an easy thing to do, I know, especially for Christians, who supposedly love God and His Word. But like most things, it's much harder than it seems."

"Absolutely, " I agreed. "You're a wise man."

Startled, Hassan did a double take.

"Hardly," he replied and rolled his eyes. "You can't really be wise about anything when you're locked up in a place like this and not really living. I mean, what do I really know about relationships?"

"Now who is being too hard on himself," I contradicted. "You still have *the light of life*, even in a place like this."

"That I do," he replied and scratched at his naked chin. "Even though it doesn't always feel like it. I know… you're right."

Chapter 20

Rehab didn't work fully. It clearly didn't do anything positive for Zoe's disposition. She called me and duly reported that she was back home and that she had the requested documentation signed by her alcohol counselor. She was short and aloof. I just thanked her for letting me know and hung up the phone as quickly as I could.

While I continued to have some compassion for her, I had long ago grown more than a little tired of her attitude. She never once showed any remorse for having driven her car into a house where children were sleeping. Nor was she the least bit grateful to her parents, who paid for her to go to rehab at that fancy place and who were also paying her legal bills. If we focus too much on our own suffering, then that's the only thing we tend ever to see.

I hadn't heard anything from Scott Truman about our civil lawsuit against Longley Insurance. The case was only four months old, so obviously, it was still fairly new. But I needed to know what they were thinking. I had hoped that we would have gotten a real settlement offer by now.

"Hi Scott, it's Sam Hicks calling about the Longley Insurance case."

"Oh, hi, Sam," Scott replied. "I have been meaning to call you."

"Really?"

"Yes, I was hoping that we could schedule your client's deposition," he said.

"Well, I don't think we finished the last one yet," I stated. "Remember, Bob Wells walked out."

"Yeah, of course I remember that," Scott replied. "I think we both know that he's a problem. I haven't been able to get the guy to call me back since he resigned."

"He quit his job?" I probed.

"Yeah, he did a few days after the deposition," he advised. "He doesn't like you very much."

"I don't think he likes you either," I contended.

"So, I'm thinking that the best thing to do is to just move on."

"Do you still represent him?" I wondered.

"Uh, I don't honestly know."

"Well, I think we need to figure that out before we do anything else," I presented. "He's a named defendant in this case, and you haven't withdrawn your representation of him."

"Sam, I know all that, but what I'm telling you is the Insurance Company doesn't want to put any money on the table until we have had a chance to depose your client under oath."

"Why?"

"Because it's the only way that we can assess what this case is worth."

"That's not really true."

"We have a right to depose her," he maintained. "You

can't hide her forever."

"I'm not hiding her," I contended. "She was at the Wells deposition."

"We know about the DWI."

"Then you know that Zoe's really messed up over what your client did to her."

"I think that we both know that her problems go much deeper than that."

"Maybe, but your client made them worse," I argued. "They did absolutely nothing to protect her from that predator."

"So say you."

"What else is there to know?" I positioned. "It's just gonna cost them more in the end to prolong the inevitable."

"That's our decision to make, not yours," Scott rebutted.

"True," I conceded. "So, how do you suggest we go forward?"

"I really wish that you would reconsider and let me depose your client without having to get the judge involved. I'm telling you that it's the easiest way for us to get you what you want."

"Not gonna happen," I declared.

"…Okay then," he answered. "Thanks for calling."

"No, problem."

Although I was still new to civil practice, I didn't believe for even a half-second that Scott was going to make a motion to the court under these circumstances. I couldn't see the insurance company approving such a costly move. Time is money for a law firm. Bob Wells walking out of the deposition was the best thing that ever could have happened for us. Scott never should have let me depose him first.

But I really wasn't sure what was going to happen next. The good thing was that I wasn't in any hurry to do anything with this case, so I was content to play it by ear and see how it went. The ball was in their court.

— • ● • —

Tony DiLauro walked into my office and sat down.

"I just got off the phone with Scott Truman," he said.

"Oh, really?" I replied. "Let me guess, he wants you to make me let him depose Zoe Carter?"

"Something like that."

"So, what did you tell him?" I wondered.

"I just want to make sure that you know what you are doing," he explained. "He says that they can't settle this case without it."

"You believe that?" I asked.

"He sounded pretty convincing."

"I'm sure he did," I condemned. "He knows that no judge is going to make me produce her when his client walked out of his own deposition."

"Are you sure about that?"

"Pretty sure," I said.

"But tell me this, what's the harm in letting him have his deposition as a sign of good faith?" Tony inquired.

"I'm not sure that I know what you mean?"

"You ever hear the phrase that you catch more flies with honey than with vinegar?"

"This is litigation," I countered. "It's not personal, at least it's not for me. I'm not sure that analogy works."

"You would know better than I would," Tony conceded and sat back in the chair. "It's just that we don't want to burn any bridges here. Utica is a small town. There will be other cases with Scott."

"As you well know, Zoe is a mess," I related. "She won't do well at a deposition, and the insurance company will low-ball us when they see that. He knows that his guy Bob Wells is a huge liability. I'm not being difficult just for the sport of it. I would never do that."

"All right," he replied. " We trust you, but I had to ask. I hope you understand."

"I do."

—•●•—

Carla and I went to the hospital to see the babies twice a day. We went every day at lunchtime and after dinner. Carly was breathing well on her own, while her brother continued to lag behind. But they were both gaining weight. They let us hold our daughter for the first time, which was very emotional for both of us. It looked like they would be coming home soon.

Overall, Carla was doing better, too. Although she still had a little right-side numbness, she was getting stronger every day. She really liked the physical therapist, and her speech was better. When she first got home from the hospital, she was dying to go to the hairdresser, and I went with her because she couldn't really drive. I think, as much as anything, that visit did wonders as far as her slow ascent toward some sense of normalcy.

But she was still fragile- remarkably so. She cried every

time she saw the babies, as soon as she laid eyes on them, and then when it was time to leave. I had no idea why she did that— she never seemed sad or conflicted beforehand. But it had become an unavoidable ritual with us that I dreaded.

One afternoon, her mother rode over with us to the hospital and witnessed her daughter having a full-blown meltdown. While consoling Carla, her eyes met mine, and I knew exactly what she was thinking. I wished that she hadn't seen it.

"Did you tell the doctor that she's still this emotional?" Mrs. Jenkins asked as soon as we got home, and we were alone.

"Yes, he knows." I took a sip of my coffee and put my cup back down on the kitchen table.

"What does he say?" she inquired and inched forward. "Is it postpartum?"

"He said that her system is still out of balance and that it's going to take time."

"But the babies are coming home soon," she stressed. "How on earth is she going to be able to handle all of that?"

"I don't know," I admitted. "I guess we will just have to cross that bridge when we get there."

"I know, but that's a pretty big bridge," she maintained

"Yeah, I know," I replied. "But a month ago, we weren't even sure that she was going to make it. Now look at her. I have to believe that we have to be patient with her. She'll find her way back. She's a fighter."

"I know you're right," she said. "I just don't know what to think anymore. But I really appreciate you, Sam, and all you do. I know that you do a lot."

She reached across the table and patted the back of my hand.

"She's so worth it," I declared.

"I'm just sorry that you have had to go through all of this," she continued. "You don't deserve any of this."

"People keep telling me that, but I'm not so sure," I said before I knew it."

"What do you mean?"

"Uh… I'm just saying maybe we shouldn't have gotten pregnant so soon."

"Honey, that's not your fault. These things just happen."

"I feel like…"

"Listen to me, please," she interrupted. "When Carla was a little girl, she had this ratty doll that she just loved. It was some cheap thing that somebody gave her, I can't remember who. It was a baby with a diaper and a bottle. She wouldn't go anywhere without it, and it got so dirty. She got mad one time when I took it and washed it, but I just couldn't take it anymore. She would love on that thing with her whole heart."

"Really?" I reacted. "She never told me about that."

"She just always wanted a baby to take care of. She's been dreaming about this for forever."

"A dream gone horribly wrong," I asserted

"I don't agree," she stated. "You guys are still just kids yourselves. You have to learn to take the good with the bad. There will always be plenty of both."

"I know," I whispered under my breath.

"Nobody blames you for anything, Sam," she said. "I didn't know that you were feeling that way. I'm sorry, I just assumed that you knew."

I didn't say anything. I stared at my coffee.

"You know, *you* saved her life," she said. "It was *you and your faith!*"

I looked up quickly.

"What?" I asked.

"You got it all wrong, Sam. We owe you! That's how I see it. That's how we all see it."

Chapter 21

It was Sunday, and I was planning to go to church, but Carla didn't want me to go. I didn't mind. It wasn't often that I got to sleep in. We decided to just spend the day together doing nothing in particular. We didn't go to visit the babies until 1:00 o'clock.

The phone rang as soon as we got home. I was taking off my coat. Carla answered it. She said it was Pastor Justin asking for me.

"Pastor?"

"Um, Sam, we have a little problem."

"What kind of problem?"

"Ah, the state police are here at my house," he advised. "They want me and Marlene to go with them to their barracks. They want to ask us some questions."

"What kind of questions?"

"About Lacey."

"What about Lacey?"

"Seems she's missing."

"*Missing* how?"

"I don't know," he replied. "What do you think we should do? Go with them?"

"Yes," I replied. "I'll meet you there. Which station?"

"Hold on, and I'll ask…He said Oneida. Do you know where that is? They want me to follow them in my car."

"Yes, I do," I assured. "I can meet you there. Don't answer any questions before I get there."

"Okay. Thanks, Sam."

He sounded worried.

"No problem. I'm leaving now."

I hung up the phone and immediately got lost in thought. I didn't like the sound of this.

"What's wrong?" Carla asked.

"Lacey, the blonde girl on the worship team, is missing."

"*Missing?*"

"The state police are looking for her."

"How long has she been missing?"

"I don't know," I replied. "They want to question the pastors about it."

"Why?"

"I'm not sure. I gotta go meet them."

I stood up and started putting my coat back on.

"Okay," she said. "Call me if you're going to be late."

"All right."

I wasn't quite sure what to think, but I had a very bad feeling. I knew Lacey was trouble. I don't know what was really going on with her husband, but my sense was that she lacked humility and couldn't be trusted. I just hoped that Pastor wasn't more involved than he said he was.

It took me about 35 minutes to get to the station. The roads were clear, and there wasn't very much traffic. I got there before them, and the sergeant on duty told me to have a seat. I admit that I was anxious, and I may have driven a little too fast.

The four of them walked in together. Two uniformed troopers led the way. They were young guys. Pastor Justin wore jeans and a blue bomber jacket, and his wife had on a black coat and black boots. They held hands. As soon as I saw them, I stood and walked in their direction.

We were taken into a conference room. There was a long wooden table with six chairs. The room was cluttered and could have used a good cleaning. The garbage can was full of food wrappers, and I just assumed that they used this room as a breakroom, too. There was a tall New York State flag in one corner and an American flag in the other.

I sat on one side of the table with my pastors. One of the troopers sat across from us. The other left the room.

"Can we have a minute?" I asked.

"Sure," he replied. "Take as long as you need."

"How are you guys?" I wondered.

"Not good," Pastor Marlene said. "I am feeling sick to my stomach."

"Do you know why they want to talk to you?"

"I guess no one has seen Lacey for a couple of days?" she reported.

"Do you know anything about that?"

"No, we don't," Pastor Justin answered.

"Well, we really can't talk here," I advised. "But is there anything that you think I should know?'

They both shook their heads.

"Okay," I said. "Listen carefully. Listen to their questions very carefully. Only answer the question that is on the table. Do not guess at anything. If you don't know for sure, then the answer is you don't know. Got it?"

"You don't think that they really think that we had something to do with Lacey going missing?' Pastor Marlene asked.

"I don't know, and that is why we have to be careful."

"I'm shocked" she exclaimed. "This is unbelievable!

"You need to calm down and put your thinking caps on. This is no time to let your emotions get the best of you."

"Are we under arrest?" Pastor Justin asked

"No, not yet."

"You think that we will be arrested?"

"I think you need to hear them out. I will be here the whole time."

They just stared at me and then at each other.

"You can do this," I reassured.

There was a knock on the door, and two different guys walked in. They were both wearing plainclothes with ties.

'Hi, I'm Investigator Jeffries, and this is Investigator Loveland. Mind if we sit down?"

He was tall and beefy with steel blue eyes. Loveland was the opposite, short and wiry.

"No, please do," I answered.

They both quickly took the two seats directly across from Pastor Justin. They both had notepads.

"Can I ask your name, Sir?" Inv. Jeffries asked.

"Sam Hicks."

"Are you a lawyer?"

"Yes, I am."

"Do you have a business card?"

I took two cards out of my coat pocket and pushed them across the table.

"Thank you," Inv. Jeffries said.

"So, can you tell me what this is about?" I questioned.

"We received a report that Lacey Stanton hasn't been seen for several days. Her

husband just returned home from a business trip, and it seems that she has disappeared.

We are trying to locate her."

"I see," I said.

"Do either one of you happen to know where Lacey is?"

"No, we don't," Pastor Justin answered.

"When was the last time you saw her?"

"Ah… probably a couple of nights ago at our church. We are her pastors."

"Yes, we know," the investigator replied. "You say you saw her at your church on Friday."

"Thursday. She was there for rehearsal with the worship team."

"Did you talk to her?"

"Not really," Pastor Justin replied. "I saw her in passing. I was there working in my office."

"What are the names of the people with who she was rehearsing ?"

"Oh, let me see… Mark White is the team leader. He was there. Sophia Wright, Pam Turner, and Colby Vincent. There may have been others, but those are the people who I recall off the top of my head."

"How did Lacey seem to you when you saw her?"

"Fine, I guess," Pastor indicated. "Like I said, I really didn't talk with her."

"What about you, ma'am? Did you talk to her?"

"I wasn't there?" Pastor Marlene said.

"Then, when was the last time you did see her?"

"About a week ago, when she was singing on the platform."

"Did you talk to her?"

"Yes, briefly."

"What did you talk about?"

"I don't really recall. It was just you know, small talk in passing."

"How long did you speak with her?"

"About a minute, or less, I'd say."

"How did she seem to you?"

"Okay. I didn't notice anything about her, but I don't really know her."

"Have you ever been to her apartment in Rome?" the investigator asked directly.

"Me? No, I don't believe so."

"Or have an argument with her about anything?"

"No," she answered.

"What about you, sir? Have you ever been there?"

"Ah… yes…yes, I have," Pastor Justin answered and cleared his throat. "Once… only one time."

"How long ago was that?"

"I can't say for sure," Pastor hedged. "Maybe a month ago."

"And why did you go there?"
"Because she called me and said that she needed to talk to me."

"About what?"

"I was counseling her for a while," Pastor Justin disclosed. "She was having

some marriage problems."

"What kind of marriage problems?"

"I'm not privy to say," Pastor recited.

"Do you normally make house calls like that?"

"No, but she said it was important. I admit that she could be a little needy."

"Do you remember what time it was? Approximately?"

"Oh… probably around 7:00 o'clock in the evening."

"Was it important?"

"To her it was."

"I don't suppose you want to tell us what that was about."

"I don't think I can."

"How long were you there?"

"About 10 or 15 minutes."

"Are you still counseling her?"

"Uh, no, I'm not."

"When did the counseling relationship end?"

"Just a few weeks ago. I can't say exactly."

"Did you call it off or did she?"

"I did."

"Why did you do that?"

"Because I thought she was getting a little too dependent on me," Pastor revealed.

"Did the two of you get into an argument that night at her apartment?"

"An *argument*? No."

"No voices were raised?"

"Not that I recall."

"How did it end?"

"I just left."

"And you never saw her again until this past Sunday."

"Yes, that's right."

"Have you spoken to her over the phone?"

"No."

"Can you think of anyone who might have wanted to harm her?"

"No, I can't."

"You work at the post office, right?"

"Yes, yes, I do."

"Have you ever met with Lacey at the post office?"

"Yes."

"When was that?"

"A couple of weeks ago."

"And you spoke to her?"

"Yes, I did. She was upset."

"About what?"

"About her husband," Pastor Justin revealed.

"Where were you when you were talking to her?"

"In the lobby."

"Did you perhaps go with her someplace a little more private, maybe to talk?"

"No, I was at work, and she showed up unannounced."

"Can you think of anything that I didn't ask you that you think might help us

to locate Lacey?"

"No."

"And you, ma'am? Can you think of anything that might help us? Anything at

all?"

"No, I'm sorry, but I can't."

"Can you excuse us for a minute?" Investigator Jeffries asked.

"Sure," I said.

The two investigators stood up together and walked out of the room. As soon as

they exited, Pastor Marlene clutched her chest, leaned toward me, and started to say something. I quickly put my hand up.

"Not now," I whispered, which startled her.

She immediately cowered, and we sat there for about five minutes without

saying a word. It seemed like longer. I had no way of knowing if they were watching us. I wasn't absolutely certain that they couldn't watch or listen in on us in their space if they were so inclined.

Inv. Jeffries walked back into the room by himself.

"I think that is all we have for now. You folks aren't planning any extended trips out of town, or anything, are you?"

"No," Pastor Justin replied. "No trips."

"Good," the investigator said. "In case we have any more questions, we know where to find you."

"No problem," I spoke as I rose to my feet. "We are willing to help you anyway that we can."

I walked with them to their car. The sun had gone down. The air was brisk and sent chills through me. I didn't want to stand there too long. I had left my overcoat in the car.

"What do you think, Sam?" Pastor Justin asked.

"They obviously know more than they were saying," I said. "They have already spoken to somebody besides the husband."

"If something bad did happen to Lacey, do you think

they would consider us to be suspects?" Pastor Justin inquired.

"Of course they do," his wife snapped. "Why else would they drag us out of our house like this on a Sunday night?"

"I don't know," he replied. "I was just trying…"

"You should have tried harder when all this stuff first started," she contended. "As far as I'm concerned, all of this could have been avoided."

"Listen," I interjected. "We're all tired and on edge right now. There really isn't much that we can do about it tonight. I think you should just go home and try to get some rest. We can talk more later."

"Did we say anything wrong?" Pastor Justin questioned. "I know how it sounded."

"You answered truthfully, right?" I reinforced. "You both did. The facts are what they are."

"Should we be worried?" Pastor Marlene interjected. "We have a family and the entire church dependent on us!"

---"Let's just pray that Lacey shows up soon," I voiced calmly. "That's really the best thing that can happen for everyone."

"You're right, of course," she echoed. We need to be praying that nothing bad has happened to her."

She pinched the bridge of her nose and looked downward to the right, confirming what I already suspected. She didn't tell the entire truth in there. I wasn't sure what to make of it because people lie for all kinds of reasons. But I was fairly certain that Investigator Jeffries didn't believe her either, by the way he leaned into her when she spoke. He was reading both of them pretty good, I'd say. This was bad.

Chapter 22

Carla wanted to know what happened with the state police as soon as I got home. I just told her that Lacey's husband reported her missing, and they wanted to talk to Pastor Justin because he was counseling her.

"She's married?"

"Yes, she is."

"You know, I hate to say it, but I always thought that something was a little off with her," Carla divulged. "I hope she's okay."

"Something like what?"

"I don't know, but I can tell that she really likes the attention of men."

"What does that mean?" I wondered. "I thought every woman wanted the attention of the opposite sex."

"Not like that," she said. "That's why I didn't think she was married. She's pretty, but in an alluring kind of way. A little too much *game,* I'd say, especially being at church."

I knew what she meant, even though I never would have put it that way. Actually, I have always thought that few men really understand women. My grandmother always said that women are smarter than men. That was part of the reason that I didn't trust Pastor Justin being around her.

Carla called me at the office early in the morning of the next day.

"Sam, you're not gonna believe this?"

"What?'

"They just found Lacey's car," she stated.

"What?" I reacted. "Who told you that?"

"Betsy from the news station just told me. You remember, Betsy. She's the one with twin boys."

"Where was it found?"

"She said Steuben County. I don't know where that is."

"It's north of Rome where she lives," I said.

"Do you think that means that somebody kidnapped her?"

"I don't know what it means," I admitted.

"I bet it was her husband," Carla surmised.

"Why do you say that?'

"Because you said that he's the one who reported her missing. He's probably just trying to cover his tracks."

"Maybe."

"Ahh…I feel bad for Lacey," Carla said.

"I probably should try to talk to Pastor," I reflected. "He's probably at work. This really is upsetting news."

"Okay, you'd better call him then," she encouraged. "The news should be public by now."

Pastor couldn't come to the phone, and I had to leave a message. I was feeling a little anxious. I just asked that he call me when he got a chance and hung up the phone. I knew him well enough that this information wasn't going to sit well with him. I needed to talk to both him and Pastor Marlene before people from the church started calling them.

On a whim, I picked the phone up again and called Paul Paolini at the district attorney's office. It took a minute before he picked up the line.

"Hi, Sam."

"Hey, Paul. I need to ask you something."

"What's that?"

"There's a woman at my church who disappeared or something from her apartment in Rome, and I just heard that they found her car somewhere in Steuben County. Do you know anything about that?"

"Sam, you know I can't comment on an open investigation."

"Yeah, I know," I replied. "I just want to know if they found Lacey in the car. She is one of our lead singers. Everyone is very concerned."

"Ah…no. There was no one in the car."

"Are they going to search the area looking for a body?"

"No, not really," he replied. "Actually, they are planning to go door to door and ask the people who live up there if they saw anything."

"They're not going to search the woods for her?"

"No, I don't believe so."

'Why not?"

"I'm not sure."

"I bet a lot of folks at the church would like to help out in any search," I threw out there.

"Just stay tuned."

"Hmm, okay," I said. "Thanks, Paul. I really appreciate it."

As I suspected, Pastor Justin had already heard the news, and he was having a bit of a meltdown when he called me an hour later. I was heading out the door to go pick up Carla to go to the hospital to visit the twins, and didn't have a lot of time to go over everything.

"Do you think she's dead?" he blurted out. "That's what everyone is saying."

"They didn't find a body."

"How do you know that?"

"Because I reached out to someone I know in law enforcement, and that's what he told me."

"Praise God!" he expressed. "That's a relief."

"Yes, it is, but that means that she is still missing and now the police know for sure that something is afoul."

"Well, of course it is," Pastor said. "Something really awful probably happened to her."

"What you are not getting, Pastor, is that from an investigatory standpoint, this is a possible kidnap - murder case."

"A what?"

"You heard me, and everyone is a suspect, including *you* and *your wife*."

"That's absurd!" he resisted. "We aren't those kinds of people."

"Everybody always says that," I maintained. "The state police don't know anything about you, but you better believe that they are going to be asking around now, looking for dirt on you both."

"But we are her pastors."

"Did you forget that her husband thinks the two of you are having an affair? Wanna guess what he told them about you?"

"We had nothing to do with this!" he protested.

"I know, but until this is all over, I need you to keep a low profile about it," I instructed.

"A low profile?"

"That means I want you to stop talking to people at your job about it or anyone else, for that matter," I requested. "I mean, no one! Not a word!"

"But isn't that going to look weird- like we're hiding something?"

"I don't care how it looks," I said. "Just tell people that you are praying for Lacey and nothing else. You can't trust anyone, and you don't want someone to set you up?'

"Why would anyone want to set me up?"

"I don't know why, and you don't know either," I stressed. "That's my point."

"But…"

"But nothing, Pastor!" I interrupted. "Just listen to what I'm telling you! This is no joke!"

"I know it's not a joke," he professed.

"Then act like it," I demanded. "The state police are looking at you for this. Do you understand? You need to be thinking about yourself and not about Lacey."

"Yes, I understand."

"Do you? Because that's not what it sounds like to me."

"Yeah…okay."

"Please call your wife," I instructed. "Tell her what I said. Everything goes for her, too."

"Okay."

"We need to meet too. The three of us. Tonight."

I only regretted slightly the way that I spoke to Pastor Justin. But it could have been a lot worse. I actually held back a lot. He was clueless.

— • ● • —

We got great news. The twins were coming home in a week. They still looked really tiny to me, especially Sampson, who now weighed in at 5lb 8oz. Both of them had their eyes open and followed our voices. We took turns holding them. It was truly magical.

"You ready for this?" I asked on the car ride home.

"I don't really have a choice," she said. "Do I?"

She was slowly becoming better composed. This was one of the few times that she didn't cry when we left the hospital.

"I think that you are going to be a great mother."

"You always think that I'm better than I really am," she stated.

"That's not true," I asserted. "I just know how strong you are."

"I don't know what you're talking about," she indicated.

"Your body carried those two miracles. Not mine. Need I remind you that *you* did that?"

"But I almost died in the process."

"Never was gonna happen," I asserted.

"My mom said you looked like death warmed over yourself most of the time."

"I wouldn't really read too much into that," I contended.

"It was an act."

"An act?" she questioned with a smirk. "Really, Sam!"

"I was just looking for a little sympathy," I maintained. "Everyone was so focused on you. I was feeling a little left out."

"Oh, you're so full of it!" she admonished.

"Speaking of which," I continued. "There is something that I probably need to tell you up front."

"What is it?"

She tensed slightly.

"Um, this is hard for me to say, so please try to be understanding," I begged. "You probably shouldn't count on me changing any diapers ever. I have a really weak stomach, and my doctor already said that it makes more sense for you to do it."

She fought hard against smiling and lost badly.

"Why are you laughing?" I asked. "I have been like this my whole life. You can even ask my grandmother. You know, I'm not making this up or anything just to get out of it. It's just that I can't see or smell stuff like that. It's a proven medical condition. You can look it up."

"I'm not looking anything up," she replied and covered her mouth and nose with both hands.

Her body shook in laughter.

"See, I knew you weren't going to be understanding," I said.

"Oh, but Sam, I do understand," she replied. "You got a week. I suggest you practice!"

———•●•———

The pastors lived in a light brown raised ranch in a modest housing development. It was across the street from an elementary school. I got lost on the way because the lighting in the area was bad and the street looped in a strange way. This was my first time being there.

"Come on in, Sam," Pastor Justin said.

He was wearing a white T-shirt, jeans, and socks. He led me up a couple of stairs into a spacious living room. There were quite a few family photos on display."

"Have a seat. Can I get you something to drink?"

"No, no I'm good."

"Marlene will be out in a minute. How's Carla?"

"Um, she's good. We were just at the hospital tonight. Looks like the babies are coming home next week."

"Hey, that's terrific! Congratulations."

"Thank you."

"Hi Sam," Pastor Marlene walked in from behind me. "Can I get you something?"

Her hair was in a ponytail. She was wearing a black sweatshirt and black pants. She had slippers on her feet, and her toes were painted a light pink color.

"No, thank you," I repeated.

She sat down on the sofa next to her husband, directly across from me.

"Did you hear, Mar? The babies are coming home next week?"

"What?" she exclaimed. "Carla must be beside herself. I'm so happy for you guys."

"Thank you," I replied. "We are very excited. It's been quite the journey for us."

"But you made it through," she pointed out and smiled

warmly. "Bless God!"

"Ah, I don't want to keep you, I know that it's getting late," I said. "So what do you say we just get right to it?"

"Yes, please," she encouraged.

"First, you should probably know that this is a criminal investigation now," I announced. "It's not just a missing person anymore. Something happened to Lacey, and it's reasonable to assume that it probably was something bad."

"Yeah, you told me that earlier," Pastor Justin remarked.

"I'm sorry, Pastor, if I was too strong with you before, but this is very serious now."

"No, problem."

"Pastor Marlene, are you sure that you have never been to Lacey's apartment?"

"Yeah, I'm sure," she replied. "Why did the police say something?"

"No, they didn't say anything to me. But my guess is that somebody told them something different."

"I don't know who that could have been," she replied.

"Me either," I stated. "But keep in mind that if the police find out that you weren't completely forthcoming with them, they are going to come back at you harder."

"Uh-huh," she sounded.

"Right now, the authorities are considering all of the possibilities, including the possibility that one or both of you are directly involved in whatever happened to Lacey."

"Why would we want to harm her?" Pastor Justin asked.

"Who knows? It could be some kind of crazy love triangle. It's one of the oldest stories ever told."

The pastors didn't say anything immediately, but I

could see them thinking.

"But how could we have done anything like that?" Pastor Justin inquired. "Where's the body? How could we hide her car like that? It doesn't make sense to me."

"Those are all valid questions," I admitted. "But they are trying to put those pieces together now."

"And I should probably say that it's not just you who they are looking at," I added.

"What should we do?" Pastor Marlene asked.

"Nothing," I advised. "Do absolutely nothing. Don't talk to anyone about Lacey."

"Okay," she said.

"The police know that they can't talk to you now without your lawyer being present. But they can talk to anybody else, including the entire church."

"They can do that?" Pastor Justin reacted.

"Yes, they can."

"And we don't know what anybody is going to say," I emphasized.

"All right," she whispered and looked at her husband.

"If this goes any further, then my advice is that you hire a lawyer."

"Not you?" he questioned.

"No, not me," I said. "For starters, my firm doesn't do criminal defense work. But more to the point, even if we did, I'm too close to this case. It would be a conflict of interest for me to represent you."

"Hmm," he uttered.

"Don't worry, I can help you find someone," I offered. "But hopefully we won't get to that point."

"Sam, before Justin called me this afternoon and told

me what you said, I want you to know that I did talk with a couple of the teachers at the school where I teach and told them that we had spoken to the police."

"What did you say exactly?"

"Just that they told us that she was missing and wanted to know if we knew where she might be. I didn't even tell them that we went to the station."

"Okay," I responded. "What's done is done. But please, not another word."

"Yes, I understand. I'm sorry."

Chapter 23

Lacey's disappearance was front-page news. The story was everywhere. There were two photographs of Lacey shown on the local news channel, one of which appeared to be from her wedding. Her husband looked different from what I imagined, more squirrelly, I'd say.

They also interviewed two women from the daycare where she worked. They mostly talked about how kind and giving Lacey is and how good she is with the children. One of them became tearful. She said that she always thought that Lacey looked like an angel.

Inv. Jeffries called me at my office.

"Good morning, Mr. Hicks."

"Good morning."

"I'm sure by now that you have heard that we have found Lacey Stanton's car?"

"Yes, I know."

"We have found several fingerprints throughout the interior of the car, and I was hoping that your clients would voluntarily come back in so that we can fingerprint them?" he inquired.

"Both of them?" I asked.

"Yes, we want to see if we can match every print we found. It's just routine."

"But they were never in the car?"

"Again, this is routine," he answered. "You know by now that we suspect foul play here. That means that the car is a crime scene."

"When would you like for them to come in?"

"Today, if at all possible. Just let me know. I can meet them at any time."

"Can I ask you a question?" I solicited.

"Sure," he replied.

"How come you guys haven't searched the woods around where you found the car? Maybe use a dog?"

"Because there weren't any tracks of any kind anywhere around the car," he surprisingly volunteered. "The ground in the area is very soft this time of year, before the deep freeze comes. Two of the tires were sunk down pretty good. There is no way that anyone could walk around that car or carry anything like a body out of there without leaving tracks. There were none."

"So, you think that the car was just dumped there?"

"Yeah, most likely," he conceded. "There were no signs of struggle inside the car, or in her apartment for that matter."

"I see," I responded. "Thanks."

I called Pastor Justin at the post office, and I had to leave a message again. But this time, he called me right back.

"Fingerprints? Are you kidding?" he complained.

"Afraid not," I said.

"They're treating us like common criminals. We've never been in Lacey's car."

"Then there's no reason to refuse, is there?" I posed.

"I'm just saying that it seems like a waste of time."

"Well, you can't really say no," I replied. "They can always get a judge to order you to submit."

"No, no, no," he objected. "We are not refusing. I didn't mean to imply that. I'm just saying that they should spend more time looking for Lacey and less time harassing us."

"I think that they would say that this is all part of looking for Lacey," I explained. "Are you available to go today?"

"We can probably go around 5 o'clock."

"Okay, I'll call him back and tell him. I can't be there because we have to go up to the hospital."

"You're not coming with us?" he questioned in a panic-filled voice.

"You don't really need me," I said. "They will just take your fingerprints. They can't talk to you or ask you any more questions without me being there."

"Okay, I'll let Marlene know, and can you just call me back and confirm the time."

"Yes, I'll do that."

At this point, I couldn't decide if this was a good turn of events for us or not. Obviously, the presence or the absence of anyone's fingerprints in the car didn't prove anything definitively. However, if someone's prints were, in fact, found inside, and that individual had previously denied ever being in the car, then that would presumably move that person to the top of the list of suspects.

Even so, Inv. Jeffries never actually asked either one of the pastors if they were ever in Lacey's car, although one would have expected that that is something that they would have mentioned on their own if they really wanted to know.

I really didn't know what to believe.

To this point, however, it was suddenly abundantly clear that I couldn't fully trust either one of them, which was a problem for me on several different fronts. I could hardly be objective. We were quickly moving closer to the point where they needed to retain their own attorney.

I reconsidered and met my pastors at the same police station in Oneida at 5 o'clock. They were very nervous again, so it was a good thing that I was there to keep them calm. We were only there about 30 minutes altogether. Thankfully, it was pretty painless.

———•●•———

As promised, the judge sentenced Zoe to three years' probation, $1,000 fine with a surcharge and restitution on her misdemeanor conviction. She was permitted to apply for a restricted driver's license that would allow her to drive to and from work. The judge wished her luck and told her that he hoped that she would get her life in order before it was too late. Zoe didn't say a word, and the sentencing itself lasted about two minutes.

I spoke with Zoe and her mother briefly after court. I wanted to make sure that they didn't have any questions.

"How long before she can get this misdemeanor off her record?" Pauline asked.

"I don't know exactly," I admitted. "That's a question for her probation officer."

"Will she have to be on probation for the full three years?"

"She can be discharged early depending on how well

she does. But she will have to pay the restitution for any damages she caused those people in full before she can be discharged from probation."

"Will that lady probation officer keep coming to my house?"

"She needed to interview you and your husband in order to write the pre-sentence report for the judge. I don't think you will have to deal with her anymore."

"Good, because I thought she was rude," Pauline said. "The way she spoke to us was uncalled for."

"What about you, Zoe?" I asked. "Do you have any questions about anything?"

"No," she whispered and twisted her hair behind her ears and rocked unsteadily on her feet.

"Well, you can call me if you do have any," I indicated. Zoe nodded her head.

Truthfully, she looked sadder than sad in that the lights had now completely gone out of her eyes. It was like she was trying to hide out in plain sight. Beauty mixed with angry pain is a lethal combination- sort of the perfect storm that only gets worse with every strong wind. Whatever medication she was taking was only taking the edge off and masking her true feelings. She was a mess…period.

Chapter 24

Two prints matching Pastor Marlene's were found inside Lacey's car. The police didn't tell me where in the car they found them. They wanted to question her again, only this time under oath. I was getting more and more concerned… and more annoyed with my shepherds.

"I didn't lie to them," Pastor Marlene stated to me on the phone when I called her.

"It most definitely *was* a lie," I reacted. "It was a lie of omission, and you know better. You knew that you had information that they needed to know, and you purposely kept it to yourself."

"They don't need to know everything about my business," she resisted. "It has nothing to do with whatever happened to Lacey."

"Maybe not, but that wasn't your call to make."

"I don't agree," she argued. "I have to look out for my family. Who else is going to do that? You?"

I felt mocked and belittled for all of my actions in helping them. But this was business for me now, not personal, and I was well able to push aside her not so subtle dismissal.

"Whether you agree or not, isn't the point," I set forth after taking a deep breath. "You have made matters a whole lot worse."

"I took a chance," she replied.

"And lost badly," I forcefully stated.

She didn't respond.

"Why were you in her car?" I continued.

"She was waiting for me one day at the school when I was leaving for the day. She drove up next to me, rolled down the window, and told me to get in. I walked around and sat in the front seat."

"What did she want?"

"Basically, she wanted me to step aside gracefully so that she and my husband could be together."

"She told you that?"

"Yes, she said that the two of them were in love, so I had already lost him."

"What happened next?" I questioned.

"I told her that she was out of her mind, and that Justin would never leave his family for the likes of her. That's when she threatened to go to Elder Dick at the church and tell him that Justin had forced himself on her."

"What?" I asked.

"Yes, she literally said that if she couldn't have him, then she would make sure that I didn't either."

"I suggested that she try explaining that to our children. She said that she didn't care anything about the kids. I said Justin cares a lot about them, and he would never trade his family for a deranged person."

"What did she have to say to that?"

"That's when she lost her mind and started screaming

and yelling at me," she related. "I jumped out of the car and told her to never come anywhere near me again. I slammed the door as hard as I could. I heard her laughing as she drove away."

"Did you tell Pastor Justin what happened?" I asked.

"No, I didn't."

"Why not?"

She didn't answer.

"You guys could communicate better," I judged. "I don't understand why you wouldn't have told him."

"Look, I know my husband," she came back. "He's a good man… a man of God. But he has certain… *weaknesses*, shall we say. I knew that he wasn't having an affair with her. I'm not being naïve. I think that most men are capable of just about anything, but not Justin. He just doesn't have any of that in him. No, she was pressuring him all right. Telling him would have just made everything worse. I was afraid of what he would have done."

"So, what did you do?"

"I thought about calling you, but you are Justin's friend," she pointed out. "He would have been angry. So, I called my good friend Sherri in Tennessee. We met in Bible College, and she and her husband Russ are pioneering a church near Memphis. She said that we should report all of this to our board immediately and beat Lacey to the punch. But I wasn't so sure about that either. I didn't want any scandal in the church. I still don't want that."

"I'm afraid that that horse has already left the barn," I declared

"I felt like we were in a no-win situation," she said soberly.

"That's when people usually do things that are out of character for them," I contended.

"Maybe, but we didn't harm her."

"Why did you go to her apartment?" I shifted.

"Oh…um… I went there to try to talk some sense into her. I actually kind of liked her before she set her sights on my husband."

"You really thought that was going to work?" I asked.

"I had to try."

"How did it go?"

"She's a coldhearted snake!" she charged. "Up there supposedly worshiping God every week! Sickening!"

"So, it didn't go well," I concluded.

"She yelled at me to get out of her house and to never come back."

"Was anyone else there?" I asked.

"Not that I saw?"

"I think that somebody either saw or heard the two of you," I advised.

"Ah, I don't know who that could be."

"Well, you are going to have to come clean with the police," I demanded. "You have to tell them about all of your interactions with Lacey. Do you understand?"

"Yes, I understand."

"Is there anything else that you want to tell me?"

"I never touched that woman."

"I believe you."

"Thanks."

"Did you have any other contact with her other than what you just mentioned?"

"No, I didn't."

"Are you sure?"

"Yes, I'm sure."

"All right then."

"I'm worried," she admitted.

It sounded like she was crying.

"God's got it," I impressed. "Believe me, I know these things."

"I know you do," she whispered through her sniffles.

———•●•———

We were at the Oneida station the next day for nearly four hours. It seemed to take Inv. Loveland forever to transcribe the two-page written statement, which thereafter Pastor Marlene had to read and sign. I felt sorry for Pastor Justin, who had to wait out in the lobby the entire time. But all things considered, I thought Pastor Marlene did well—much better than the first time.

I wasn't just being kind. I didn't see any way that Pastor Marlene could have been involved in Lacey's actual disappearance, at least not by herself. She probably only weighed about 100 pounds soaking wet. The biggest problem is that we didn't have all of the information that the state police had. As expected, they were careful not to tip their hand.

But Pastor Marlene's statement directly implicated her husband. If Lacey was, in fact, pressuring him to leave his wife and threatening to expose him using lies, then he definitely had a motive for wanting to harm her. And unlike his wife, he could have easily overpowered Lacey and moved her body somewhere.

However, at this point, there were just too many unknowns. I suspected that the police still felt that way, too. The worst thing that could happen from our perspective would be for Lacey's body not to be found because important evidence, such as the cause of death and wound marks, cannot be considered.

To be clear, a person can be convicted of murder even if the victim's remains are never recovered. It's often much easier to establish *proof beyond a reasonable doubt* in a court of law than one might otherwise think, depending upon who is on trial and the strength of the circumstantial evidence.

That is, indirect evidence can send an accused person to prison for the rest of his or her life. The key, in such instances, is proof of motive and opportunity to commit the crime. Pastor Justin arguably had both, even if his wife didn't.

I was dying to know what was going on with Lacey's husband, who clearly had a motive as well. Others had to know that theirs wasn't the perfect marriage. Pastor Justin told me that her husband, Michael, was a truck driver who was gone a lot on the road. If he was physically abusive to Lacey, as she claimed in her counseling sessions, then the authorities had to be looking hard at him as well. One could reasonably assume that his fingerprints would have been somewhere in Lacey's car, too.

One thing I really missed was working with other lawyers whose opinions I trusted. I ended up calling Jim

McCaffrey, a criminal attorney in town whom I first met when I was at the public defender's office. He was an excellent criminal attorney and a good guy.

"Jim, you probably heard about the young woman from Rome who has been missing now for over a week?"

"Yes, I have."

"I know her," I indicated. "We go to the same church."

"Sorry to hear."

"The state police had the pastors come in for questioning. I went with them. I think that there are some problems for them because they were having some serious issues with this woman."

"What kind of *issues*?"

"It's complicated … suffice it to say she may have been aggressively pursuing some kind of romance with the pastor."

"I see," Jim commented.

"Obviously, I can't represent them."

"No, you can't," he affirmed.

"I was hoping that this might be something that you might consider taking if he gets charged?"

"Sounds interesting," he expressed.

"If you were to get involved, when would you like to meet them?" I wondered.

"It doesn't sound to me like they are close to charging anyone," he opined. "They haven't found a body yet. Obviously, we don't know when or if that will happen."

"Right."

"The investigation will probably go on for quite a while. As long as you are representing them… er, looking out for them… I think that you can keep advising them the way that you have been doing. That would definitely save them some money and aggravation. They don't know me like they do you. Um…I would want to be called as soon as an arrest is made, or you definitely know that that is going to happen."

"Anything that I should be focused on now?" I questioned.

"No, not really," he concluded. "I'm confident that you know what you are doing. But if I were you, I wouldn't fully trust that the pastor is telling you everything."

"I don't," I reluctantly admitted.

"Don't allow the state police to question him anymore unless they have a really good reason for wanting to do so. And then limit what they can ask him. If they come back again, it's probably not a good sign."

"Got it," I replied. "That helps. Thank you."

"Thank you for thinking about me," Jim said. "I'm very flattered. Hopefully, I won't hear back from you about this, and everything will just work itself out. That's what typically happens."

"I can't thank you enough," I replied.

Ultimately, it was very reassuring to me to know that I wasn't really missing anything because I wasn't sure. Pastor Justin was suddenly having a hard time relating to me, and it was awkward between us. That was never the case before. Sometimes it's easier to tell our secrets to a perfect stranger than it is to tell them to someone we know personally. This was hard for both of us.

Chapter 25

Jeff Parella, a probation officer from the Oneida County Probation Department, called me about Zoe. I was out of the office, and he left a message for me to call him. He said it was important, but not necessarily urgent.

"Hi, Jeff."

"Sam the man!"

"How are you?" I asked.

"I'm good, man. How are you now that you have moved on up to the eastside?"

"Still the same old grind, brother!"

"But at least they pay you better for it."

"True."

"Sam, you represented Zoe Carter, right?"

"Yes, I did."

"The reason why I'm calling is to let you know that she's not really adjusting to probation very well."

"How so?"

"You know me, I don't ride my people. As long as you play it straight with me, it's all good. But she's not even trying. She doesn't show up for our meetings on time, and she seems to be zoned out when she gets here. I drug tested her, and she's okay for now. But either she doesn't fully get why she is here, or she's just playing games."

"I'm sorry to hear that," I replied.

"I don't want to violate her," he admitted. "She's only been on probation like a month. But I will if she doesn't get her act together. I can't fully assess what other resources she needs because she's so detached."

"I think she's depressed," I offered. "She was like that with me, too."

"You need to talk to her, bro."

"Yeah, but what do I say?" I asked. "I'm pretty much at a loss, too."

"Tell her that I'm a real son of a gun and that I'll send her butt to jail in a heartbeat if she doesn't get it together."

"Right."

"She denies being depressed," he reported. "Probably because she doesn't want to take the medication. A lot of them play that trick."

"Okay, I'll tell her and do what I can," I pledged. "Thanks for letting me know."

"No problem."

I really had no idea what to do with Zoe. Obviously, she was crying out for help. If she was in this much pain, then it was only a matter of time before she started drinking again, if she hadn't already. That would be a violation of her probation, too, and she could be sent to jail for a year.

This kind of thing was common with the people whom I used to represent in the public defender's office. I had gotten used to clients sabotaging their plea deals for quick fixes to escape their pain, like alcohol and drugs. Back then, I knew that there wasn't much that I could do as appointed counsel, who didn't really have their attention or respect. So, I seldom tried to do anything.

I called Zoe's parents and requested a meeting with them at my office - just the three of us. I felt like a high school principal demanding to speak to the difficult parents of a juvenile delinquent. I definitely wasn't looking forward to it, but I was sick of their garbage.

Honestly, I wasn't even sure what I was going to say to them. While I didn't know for certain whether they were to blame, in whole or in part, for Zoe's self-destructive behavior, it was obvious to me that whatever they were doing to help her wasn't working. They were clearly just as lost as their daughter was.

They arrived together on time. I couldn't read their moods, but I just told myself that this wasn't really about the two of them. I was tired of listening to them dance around each other while Zoe drifted further away. Although I was definitely a little nervous myself, I was intent on putting a stop to the overall madness.

"Um, according to Zoe's probation officer, she is not doing well," I began.

"In what way?" Joe Carter asked.

"In just about every way," I responded. "She's halfheartedly going through the motions and detached. She resents being there, and she's not taking it seriously."

"We know," Pauline acknowledged.

"Well, if she doesn't change her attitude quickly, he said that he is going to kick her out of probation."

"He can do that?" Pauline questioned.

"Yes, he can do that," I replied. "And if he does, that means that she will be resentenced, and the judge can send her to jail for up to a year."

"A year?" Joe repeated to himself and groaned.

"Yes, a year."

"I knew this was going to happen," Pauline chimed in. "She had to move back home with us for financial reasons. I think that was kind of the last straw for her."

"Well, I can tell you that going to jail for that long will be a new low for her, one that she might not ever come back from," I contended. "It will completely rob her of any dignity she has left."

"Oh my God!" Pauline exclaimed.

Zoe's parents looked at each other, and then a quiet hush began to fill the room. I just looked straight ahead and let them feel the full weight of it.

"My wife just had twins last month who are preemies," I revealed. "It's a long story, but a part of me was afraid to meet them after they were born because I was worried that I wasn't… you know… ready to love them right ... But it turns out that I was only partly right. When I held my daughter for the first time, it was like a veil was lifted, the sun shone through, and I got a glimpse of the very face of God for the first time."

"How wonderful for you," Pauline expressed.

"I already love my kids more than I ever knew was possible, and we haven't even brought them home from the hospital yet. The love that I have for them is so much bigger than both me and my wife combined because God molded them from our love. There is almost nothing that I wouldn't do for them."

My voice began to break. They both looked at me intently.

"I would die for them right now if I had to," I professed. "I swear that I would. Have either one of you ever felt like that?"

Pauline's face lit up. She uncrossed her legs and leaned forward.

"When Zoe was born, I remember feeling the same way," she said and smiled to herself. "I felt like I finally had someone whom I could pour out all my love on. You know, someone of my very own. I had been waiting my whole life for this."

"What happened?" I asked. "When did it change for you?"

Her eyes got big, and she jolted upright.

"I don't think I know what you mean?"

"Zoe needs your love, now more than ever before," I entreated.

"I do love her with everything that I have," she answered defensively.

"She's drowning in guilt and shame," I insisted.

"I know she is."

"Then tell her father what happened to her," I said.

"What?" she reacted.

"He loves her too and needs to know… for Zoe."

"What's he talking about?" Joe wondered. "Pauline?"

She had a stunned look on her face.

"I…I... don't know," she lied.

Her eyes darted back and forth. I abruptly rose to my feet.

"Excuse me," I said. "I'll give you guys your privacy. I will be down the hall if you need me."

I walked out and closed the door behind me. My heart

rate was elevated, and I was perspiring lightly on my forehead. I knew that there was a chance that I had completely overstepped my boundaries and possibly detonated an atomic bomb in the midst of their family dynamics. But I did it for my client. I felt I had to do it for her.

I waited fifteen minutes and walked back to my office door. I thought I heard their raised voices inside, so I decided to give them a few more minutes. The truth was that I wasn't in any hurry to go back in there.

I knocked quietly on the door twice and opened it. They were both still seated, but it appeared that their chairs were moved further apart. Pauline was turned slightly away from him, and she was picking the lint from her sweater. She didn't look directly at me.

"How's it going in here?" I asked as I took my seat behind my desk.

Both of them had tear-stained faces. The tension in the room was palpable.

"Ah, is this probation officer planning to violate her now?" Joe inquired.

"No, he wants to try to work with her."

"Work with her, how?" he wondered.

"She's suffering from depression," I stated. "There are resources available."

"You think I should call him?"

"Yes."

"What's his name?"

"Jeff Parella."

"What else… do you think we should do?" he inquired.

"Anything and everything you can," I advised. "She

needs you both. That's the point. You need each other to get through."

He nodded.

"Your daughter deserves a shot at life," I uttered.

"Is there anything else that you want to say to us?"

"No, there isn't."

"Okay, let's go," he spoke softly without looking directly at his wife.

They got up together, grabbed their coats, and walked out both with their heads held down.

Chapter 26

Carla loved talking about Lacey's disappearance. She was caught up in all of the idle gossip and rumors. Apparently, many people had called the news station with purported information about the case, including complaints about the way law enforcement was handling the investigation. One guy reported that Lacey had been kidnapped by aliens, and she was now living in the woods behind his house.

Pastor Justin led the entire church in a prayer for Lacey's safe return. I looked around and saw that many people were crying. From where I was sitting, I could only see the back of Pastor Marlene's head. But I seriously doubted that she was shedding any tears.

Carla and I were leaving church when Elder Dick tapped me on the shoulder from behind."

"Hey Sam, might I have a word?"

He was a slight man with rough skin, deep-set eyes, and a warm smile. He was unofficially everyone's *"grandfather"* in the church.

"Oh, sure," I replied.

"I'm gonna go talk to Pam," Carla said.

"Okay," I replied.

Elder Dick and I walked a few feet together where no one could hear us.

"Sam, a few days ago, two state police guys came to see me at my house."

"Really?"

"They wanted to ask me some questions about Lacey and Pastor."

"What kind of questions?"

"They wanted to know if I knew anything about Pastor Justin and Lacey being…together… you know."

"What did you tell them?"

"I said that I didn't know anything about that."

"Did they ask you anything else?"

"They wanted to know if Lacey had ever talked to me about it," he revealed. "I was very surprised, to say the least. I'm pretty sure that I'm the last person she would have told something like that."

"Why do you say that?" I asked.

"Because I know her husband."

A wave of energy suddenly hit me. But I hid it.

"How do you know him?" I wondered.

"I've known Mikey since he was a little boy," he replied. "We're not related or anything, but I used to bowl with his daddy and Uncle Gus in my younger days. You can kinda say I know the family."

"What kind of guy is he?"

"Who, Mikey?"

"Yeah."

"Um… he was always kinda shy and quiet, I'd say," he opined. "Devin told me one time that Mikey was too soft and let Lacey carry around his testicles in her purse."

"People are saying that he was beating Lacey," I presented.

"A lot of folks around here are making up stuff just to make it seem like they are in the know," he responded in a huff.

"I know they are."

"My daughter used to say that the only reason Lacey married Mikey was that she could boss him around," he remarked and chuckled to himself. "She could have any guy she wanted, you know. It's always been that way."

"Maybe he just got tired of her being the boss," I suggested.

"He didn't beat her," he doubled down. "The boy ain't got it in him, I tell ya. More like the other way around. Trust me, she's the brains of that operation."

"Interesting," I said.

"For what it's worth, I never thought she should have been on our worship team here at the church either. She's just too *worldly*… got a bad mouth on her."

"Did the state police ask you anything about their relationship or their marriage?"

"No, he didn't ask me anything about that, just this nonsense about Pastor and her. But a lot of people know."

"I'm sorry," I shifted. "You wanted to ask me something, and I started interrogating you."

"No, that's all right," he reassured. "I was just wondering if Pastor knows what the troopers are saying about him and her. A lot of our people are hearing it."

"Uh, yes, unfortunately, he is aware of the rumors," I disclosed.

"Ugh!" he exclaimed. "I hate that it has come to this. Tell him for me that none of us believes that garbage."

"I will."

"I wonder how all this talk got started anyway," he said. "Some people ain't got nothin better to do than sit around and try to tear down the man of God."

"I know," I replied. "It's sad, really."

"You know, I'm the one who got Lacey started coming here to this church in the first place," he revealed. "I feel a little bad about that now. Those two just seem to breed trouble."

— • ● • —

I wasn't just concerned about the pastors, but I was worried about the church as well. The people were obviously great, and they really rallied around us when Carla was pregnant and when she was in the hospital. Also, I felt like I was still growing spiritually, which is the most important thing, of course. Carla and I always looked forward to the teachings, and we talked about them at length at home. It was a good fit all around.

But a part of me wished that I was just a regular member who got to sit and listen every Sunday and then go home and not think about the place again for the rest of the week. I wasn't really prepared to have to help carry the weight of the people. Although I didn't have an official title, everyone treated me like I did.

Pastor Justin was avoiding me. His wife called me twice during the past week to see if I had heard anything from the state police. But nothing from him. I thought he looked tired on Sunday. I just figured that he needed space and knew where to find me if he needed me.

Inv. Jeffries called me. He wanted to question Pastor Justin again.

"Why?" I boldly asked.

"Just some follow-up," the investigator replied.

"About what?" I pressed. "This is weighing heavily on him now. I'd like to avoid all of the back and forth if at all possible."

"We need clarification on his relationship with Lacey Stanton," he explained. "There is reason to believe that they are much *'closer'* than it first seemed."

"Under oath?" I inquired. "You want a written statement from him, too?"

"No, we don't think that will be necessary. Just a few more questions."

"How long will it take?"

"Not long."

"Okay, let me call him and get back to you."

I dreaded having to make the call. The thought occurred to me that perhaps one of the reasons why he was being so distant from me was that he was associating me with all of this stuff with the state police.

I told him everything that Inv. Jeffries had said. We decided to go in for the interview the next morning and to drive there together. I picked him up at his house.

"So, what do you think this is really about?" he asked.

He looked anxious.

"I think that they have heard all of the rumors and want to ask you about them."

"What rumors?"

"That you are having an affair with her."

"And I have to answer all of their questions?"

"Yes, as long as your answer isn't incriminating," I explained.

"I don't know what that means," he contended.

"It means that you don't have to tell them where the body is buried."

"I don't know where any body is buried."

"There you go," I commented. "That's your answer."

"And we were not having an affair," he stated emphatically.

"You know that an affair doesn't just have to be physical. It can be emotional too. What would you call it then?"

"Something very different," he insisted.

"What were you doing with her exactly?" I squeezed.

"I already told you this, too," he protested.

"I'm asking you now for the dirty details you keep omitting. I just don't want any more surprises."

"I just wanted to help her," he asserted. "It's all I ever wanted, I swear."

"But that wasn't enough for her?" I surmised. "Was it?"

"No, no, it wasn't."

"What happened?"

"Eventually, I gave up and just wanted her to leave me alone," he explained. "I told her that repeatedly. She wouldn't take no for an answer."

"She wanted a physical relationship, and you didn't?"

"Right."

"Just tell me what happened," I insisted.

"I never slept with her."

"What did you do with her exactly?"

"She uh used her hand… and started rubbing my area… you know… through my pants at first and um…"

He stopped talking and put his head down.

"Where did this happen?" I demanded.

"When she came to my job… in my car."

"Why did you get in the car alone with her?"

"I didn't want anyone to hear us talking," he explained. "She can be loud and unruly."

"So, you misrepresented yourself before when you told them that you only spoke to her in the post office lobby that day."

"Yes, yes, I did," he said quietly and looked down and away.

"I'm sorry, but I don't understand how you let something like this happen," I decried. "You said it yourself, she can't make you do anything that you didn't want her to do."

Pastor slowly lifted his head to stare directly into my eyes. He didn't say anything. He didn't have to; he let his dying eyes do the talking.

I heard every word and felt the weight of them, which was suffocating.

"Okay," I replied soberly. "Okay."

— • ● • —

It was harder this time sitting there while Inv. Jeffries interrogated my pastor. He asked detailed questions about what happened in the car that day with Lacey, which probably wasn't really necessary. Pastor answered all of their questions calmly and to the point. He never once looked to me for support. But he was being tortured slowly. I was, too. It was excruciating.

"Did you have any contact with Lacey after this incident?" Inv. Jeffries asked.

"Just over the phone," he replied. "She called me a couple of times. I told her that I wasn't interested in talking to her anymore about anything. I kept hanging up on her."

"How did she respond to you not talking to her?"

"She was angry," Pastor said. "She left me a note under my office door that said that if I was going to treat her like a whore then I needed to pay her like one."

"Do you still have that note?"

"No, I threw it away because I didn't want my wife to find it."

"Did she ask you for money specifically?"

"No, but her husband did."

"How much money did he ask for?"

"Ten thousand dollars."

"Did he ask for that in writing by chance?" he probed. "Give you some kind of a note?"

"No, he called me at the post office?"

"What did he say exactly?"

"That either I paid him ten thousand dollars, or he was going public with what I was doing with his wife."

"How did you respond?"

"I didn't," Pastor Justin replied. "I just hung up the phone on him, too. I don't have that kind of money. I didn't know what to do."

"Why didn't you tell us about this before?" Inv. Jeffries pressured.

"Because I was embarrassed, and it doesn't have anything to do with what happened to Lacey."

"We have no way of knowing that," the investigator insisted.

"I had nothing to do with her disappearance!" Pastor erupted. "I keep trying to tell you people!"

"Well, frankly, you have said, and not said, a lot of things," the investigator shot back. "We are just trying to find out what happened to this woman. No one is interested in your sex life or in embarrassing you."

Pastor didn't respond. He just hid within.

"How many times did Michael Stanton contact you altogether?"

"Twice. The first time was when he demanded that I stop seeing Lacey, and the last time was when he wanted the money."

"Do you have anything in writing from either one of them?"

"I already said no to that question."

"Uh, did you tell Lacey that Mike had called you and demanded that you stop seeing her?"

"Yes, I did."

"And how did she respond?"

"She just said to ignore him. She said that he was harmless."

"Did you tell her about the money? That Mikey wanted money?"

"No, I had stopped talking to her altogether at that point."

"One last thing, Pastor Henderson," Inv. Jeffries prefaced. "Did Lacey tell you that she is pregnant?"

"Pregnant?" he reacted as his whole body came to attention.

"Yes, her doctor has confirmed that she is pregnant."

"…Uh, no… she never told me that she is pregnant," Pastor stated in obvious shock. "That doesn't make any sense."

"What doesn't make sense?"

"Because it just doesn't," Pastor insisted.

His breath shook.

"Since you are counseling her, any idea who the father might be?"

"Her husband, I would presume," Pastor answered defensively.

"Not likely. He can't medically have children."

"Oh…then no," Pastor said and hesitated. "I don't have any idea."

"You sure she never mentioned anyone? Anyone at all?"

"No, never!" Pastor answered.

"Okay, then. That's all we have for you today."

The ride to Pastor's house from the police station was painful for us both. Embarrassment coiled around him. The silence that came with it was thick and heavy as black smog and had a choke hold on me. I could hear my heart beating along with the sound of the wind hitting the outside of the car. I felt powerless. So, I never said a word.

Seemingly, it took forever to get there. I slowly pulled into his driveway and put the car in park. I was afraid to look directly at him and studied him out of the corner of my eye. Instead, I waited for him to make the next move. It took him about a minute.

"I owe you an apology," he quietly said.

"You don't owe me anything," I replied.

"Thank you for saying that, but you're wrong," he insisted. "I know that I hurt

you because you think that I don't respect you as an equal. That's not true at all, at least not the way you mean. As your pastor and your friend, you expected more from me… and rightly so. I let you down, and I want you to know that I am very sorry."

I was uncomfortable and just kept looking straight ahead.

"The truth is that our sinful humanity has a way of clouding the already broken lens through which we all see the world we live in, ultimately impacting the way we act and think," he explained.

"Pastor, I appreciate this but…"

"Sam, one thing I know with absolute certainty is that from the day that we accept Jesus as our personal savior, until the day that we die and our spirits leave this earth, we are all *coming out of darkness* because none of us fully arrive on this side of paradise. It's true for everybody, rich or poor, Black or white or whoever. There are no free passes, not even for those of us in the ministry. God made us the same… We're all the same in His sight. Do you understand?"

"Yes, I think so," I expressed.

"Good… I'm sorry that I hurt you," he repeated.

"Pastor, what are you going to do?"

"Ah, good question," he said. "I don't really know. But right now I'm going to go into my house and beg the woman I love to forgive me too. I don't really care about much of anything else at the moment."

He glanced in my direction and briefly touched my upper arm. He then turned, opened the door, and got out of the car. He didn't look back. I watched him walk up the driveway and go into the house.

241

Chapter 27

Dr. O'Connor decided that only Carly was ready to come home. Sampson was still showing signs of irregular breathing. They wanted to keep him for another week, just to be on the safe side. We were a little hesitant to separate them, but the doctor reassured us that the babies wouldn't be aware that the other one wasn't there.

"Look at it this way," the doctor said, "It's a chance for you both to start getting used to having an infant in the house. You're in for quite the adjustment."

He was right. We were both up all night the first night home with Carly. The baby was fine; she was only fussy when she was hungry. She mostly just ate and slept. However, we were so worried about something happening to her that we couldn't sleep ourselves. I was convinced that I was going to break the baby with my big ol' hands. We really were out of our minds!

But I could tell that Carla was going to be a natural once she stopped overthinking everything. Deep down, she was very excited and wanted to prove herself. My grandmother initially came over every day, which was a big help. It allowed Carla to sleep a little while I was at work and also permitted us to keep up our hospital visits with Sampson. There were a lot of moving parts, but we managed to figure everything out.

Carla officially gave notice at her job that she would not be returning. I thought it was going to be harder on her than it actually turned out to be. She loved the people there. But she had talked it through with her counselor and seemed ready to turn the page to becoming a full-time mother.

I could see that Carla's family had every intention of being fully engaged with our children, despite the two-and-a-half-hour drive from the Rochester area, and I couldn't have been more thrilled. Carla already had to stop them from buying so much stuff. Because I had no extended family of my own to speak of, I really wanted that for my kids. I saw family as being integral to the development of a healthy sense of community and belonging in young people. That was another thing that my heart always ached for.

———— • ● • ————

Notwithstanding my many absences from work, my practice was starting to grow. Owing mostly to Tony DiLauro's connections, we somehow managed to land a deal to be outside counsel for two small local companies, which just meant that we were contracted to handle all of their defense work if they got sued by someone. It provided a steady stream of work for me, so I no longer had to worry about being able to produce for the law firm or provide for my family. It was a real blessing.

Scott Truman finally reached out to me, and made Zoe Carter a settlement offer. After minimal haggling, the insurance company was willing to pay her what amounted to a little over two years' salary. They also agreed to pay her attorney fees. I thought it was a pretty good deal for Zoe, especially since she was in no condition emotionally to fight them.

I called and explained everything to her. I probably should have met with her in person rather than discussing the private details of a settlement over the phone, but frankly, I was in no mood to wrestle with her demons. The spirit of depression is contagious, and I couldn't afford to get sick just now.

I explained to her that she would have to sign a confidentiality agreement, meaning she had to keep the terms of the settlement confidential. She asked what I thought, and I told her that it was a fair deal, although she could probably get a little more money if she wanted to play hardball and string the case out a bit longer. But I advised against it because sooner or later, she would have to sit for a deposition. She wanted time to talk to her father.

———•●•———

It was being reported in the news that a body was found in the Adirondack Mountains on a remote hiking trail and that it could possibly be Lacey's remains. Pastor Justin called me to see if I had heard anything. I told him that it was doubtful that the police would call me with any kind of an update unless they needed something from us. We just had to wait and see.

Turns out that the body they found wasn't Lacey's after all, but that of a missing man who apparently had committed suicide. This was mostly a relief – but not entirely. My prayer was that Lacey be found alive. But if she was, in fact, dead, then her body would be recovered soon so that we could all get closure.

At this point, I was fairly certain that the pastors were not involved in whatever happened to her. But the only way to fully call off the dogs and end the wild speculation running rampant throughout the community about our church was to locate her. Nobody would want to have to live under a cloud of suspicion for a prolonged period of time. Most of our people were staunch supporters of our leadership. But not everyone.

One criticism that I heard, or rather Carla heard and readily passed along to me, was that no one from our church had reached out to Lacey's husband to see if there was anything that we could do for him during this crisis. Typically, our congregation was very supportive of people in need, particularly someone in our own membership. However, there was nothing typical about this situation. If asked, my best legal advice would have been for the pastors, and everyone else, for that matter, to avoid Michael Stanton like the plague.

Pastor Justin called me again.

"Sam."

"Yes."

"Do you think it would be a problem if Marlene and I went away for a week?" he solicited. "We need some time together to sort through some things in our marriage, and we can't do it here with everything that is going on."

"Where will you go?" I asked.

"We know a marriage counsselor in Tulsa, Oklahoma,"

he replied. "We would go through an intensive with her."

"That sounds like a good idea," I said.

"We actually talked about doing this last year, but it's always hard to find the right time."

"And what about the church?" I wondered.

"We'll get a guest speaker for Sunday," he asserted. "I already reached out to someone. Then we'll just go from there. Neither one of us feels much like teaching. My heart just isn't in it, I'm sorry to say."

"Well, then by all means go," I encouraged. "I would just need a way to get a hold of you."

"Of course," he said. "Marlene's parents are coming up from Florida to stay with the boys. Both kids love it when their grandparents visit because Marlene's dad made a ton of money before he retired from NASA as a manufacturing engineer, and they love to spoil their only grandchildren. They will also know how to reach us."

"When will you leave?"

"Hopefully, Friday. I haven't bought the plane tickets yet because I wanted to wait to talk to you."

"I appreciate that, Pastor, but you are free to leave the state."

"Okay then, I will call you when we get there with the phone number."

"Sounds good," I responded. "Try not to worry about anything."

"Honestly, I'm not worried about the state police anymore," he emphasized. "It goes much deeper than that for me now."

"I know it does, Pastor," I commiserated.

I wished that there was something more that I could

have done for him — something that would have effectively eased the debilitating pain in his soul. Whatever his *weaknesses* are, as his wife so delicately put it, he definitely needed to address them. Although, admittedly, Carla and I were still newlyweds with a lot to learn about committed love in marriage, I couldn't imagine something like this ever happening to us.

— • ● • —

According to yet another newspaper story, Lacey ended up in foster care when she was just eight years old. Her young mother had a lot of problems, along with several children whom she couldn't take care of. The siblings were separated, and Lacey ultimately landed in a troubled home where the father was subsequently arrested for unspecified abuses. She was a troubled teen who purportedly turned her life around after graduating from community college. No one would have suspected her ugly past to look at her.

My guess was that Lacey told Pastor Justin all about her tortured youth in the system. No doubt, the fact that she was so broken was part of the appeal for him. The truth is that many ministry leaders are highly susceptible to a sad story, which is probably a job requirement of sorts and a good thing.

However, Pastor was right; I, for one, never cared to know anything about Lacey. In fact, I barely gave her a second thought until he told me that her husband had threatened him. I didn't even know her last name. But I probably had more in common with her than Pastor did in terms of growing up with the absence of parental affection and self-esteem.

But we were a small church, and most people now seemed to feel close to her. Worship music is essential to fundamental Christian services. For some people, it is the most important part, more than even the teaching and preaching. People generally looked up to the worship leaders. To me, her voice was just average.

Although I thought some of the stuff they wrote in the latest newspaper article was incredibly intrusive, I seriously doubted that anyone in our church thought any less of Lacey. Ironically, her abrupt departure from our midst had elevated her stature in the church and made her more beloved than ever before, something of a mixed blessing.

We specifically prayed for her by name in every service, which seemed to cast a dark cloud on everything else that came after. I really thought that everyone now believed that she was, most likely, dead. I know I did. From that standpoint, it probably wasn't the best time for our senior pastors to be out of town when so many were already grieving.

The guest speaker was Pastor Russ Teachout from Tennessee. He reminded me a little of Pastor Justin with a southern accent, although he wasn't nearly as charismatic or handsome as our pastor. The two men were about the same age, and both used a lot of humor.

He entitled his message, *"Hope for the Hopeless,"* which ended up being very inspirational. Just before he closed, he exhorted:

Dear ones, our hope is not in anything that is flesh or carnal. That is, it's not in our husband or wife, mother or father, doctor or nurse, pastor, prophet, or best friend. Our problems will come, and they

will go—that's for certain. But these things are all temporary. The

Bible tells us to fix our eyes on the things we cannot see. Man is

the only creature who has the ability to see and imagine what

could be. That means that we all have the capacity right now,

right in this moment, in the middle of your storm, to see completely

beyond it. We were first saved by faith in the hope of the

eternal God, who none of us has ever seen, but who has promised

that He will one day wipe away every tear from our eyes, and that

death shall be no more, neither shall there be mourning or crying or

pain anymore. In your heart, you know what I say is the truth. And

I'm telling you that if you catch a vision, just a glimpse of the

invisible today, it will change you for the rest of your life. So

everyone, right where you are, close your eyes. Take a deep

breath, cast your cares upward, and rest in Him…

The message was well received, and I, for one, left there feeling revived. Indeed, it was probably just what the doctor ordered for me to hear.

Chapter 28

They found Lacey alive. She was in Seattle, Washington. The local news reporter only said that she was found safe and that law enforcement thanked the public for all the help provided in locating her. No other information was given.

According to Carla, Lacey was found with her boyfriend. She also heard that Lacey's husband knew where she was the whole time. He was just embarrassed because he found out that she was having an affair. This development left many of us feeling used and angry.

I called Inv. Jeffries first thing the next morning. He wasn't in the office, so I left a message for him to call me, which he did later in the afternoon.

"I was hoping you could tell me a little more than what's being reported about Lacey," I solicited.

"Yeah, I figured that I would be hearing from you." Inv. Jeffries said.

"I have to say that I have mixed feelings about all of this," I acknowledged.

"We all do," he admitted. "These people cost the taxpayers a whole lot of time and money."

"What's it all about?" I asked directly.

"Apparently, Lacey has been seeing this guy, whom she met in a bar, for about six months. He's a real dirtbag who just got off parole. All of a sudden, she just packed up her things and left town with him without telling anyone."

"Why would she do that?"

"Who knows?" he posed. "Maybe it's true love."

"And her husband?"

"Another deadbeat," he offered.

"Why do you say that?" I questioned.

"Because we think she left him a note or something, but he denies it," Inv. Jeffries divulged. "He hid her car and pretended that she was missing just so that we would help him find her."

"Are you kidding me?" I asked in amazement. "Tell me that didn't really happen!"

"You can't make this stuff up," he replied. "We always knew that he wasn't telling the truth about everything, and he kinda sent us on a wild goose chase. There was no sign of anything amiss in their apartment, and nobody in the building saw or heard anything. It looked like she had just gone on vacation. She took her toothbrush and makeup."

"So that's the real reason why you guys didn't conduct a search in the area where you found the car?"

"Yes, sorry."

"I get it," I spoke.

"We confirmed that Mike was out of town for the three days before he reported her missing. He refused to take a lie detector. He's got himself this piece of crap lawyer, no offense, who gave him a lot of bad advice, in my opinion. But Mike Stanton was always our primary suspect, not your clients."

"How did you find out about this other guy?"

"We got a ton of leads from all kinds of people," he advised. "Most of them were loony tunes. But the owner of this dive bar in Rome called us out of the blue, and reported that he thought that one of their bartenders was seeing her. This bartender, his name is Tanner Jenson, suddenly quit his job around the same time that Lacey went missing, and no one has seen him since. We started looking for him."

"How did you find them?"

"As luck would have it, he got a speeding ticket in the State of Washington."

"Have you spoken to Lacey?"

"No, not me. But she told the investigator in Seattle that she wanted to start a new life and not have her baby in New York. It's doubtful that she'll ever show her face here again."

"I don't know what to say," I replied, dumbfounded.

"For what it's worth, we think that they were planning to extort money from your guy, the pastor, all along."

"Why do you say that?"

"Because Mike never called the pastor and demanded money," he related. "He didn't really even know what church Lacey went to or anything about the pastor. It was all news to him. That's one thing that he was actually telling the truth about. No, we believe that this Tanner is the one who made those calls to your guy."

"Then the stuff that happened in the car at the post office was a setup," I said. "Yeah, I'd say," he agreed. "She needed to get him to cross the line with her so

that she had something on him, more than a little kiss. She knew he liked her. Predators like her smell *weakness*."

"What about charging them with extortion?"

"No money was ever exchanged," he pointed out. "It's weak—his word against hers. I guess you know that better than I do."

"Hmm," I begrudgingly concurred.

"At least, their names have been cleared," the investigator asserted.

"I don't think that's going to make them feel any better," I contended.

"No, I suppose not," he agreed.

"Hard to accept being blindsided like this," I said. "Nobody at the church ever did anything to her but welcome her and treat her like one of the family."

"Obviously, everything I just told you is unofficial," he added. "But I think that you folks have a right to know."

My heart was racing when I hung up the phone. I had to force down a sick feeling. The harsh reality was that Pastor Justin was groomed by a perverted soul, who mercilessly turned against him and ripped out his heart.

In a way, that's what happened to Jesus, who wanted only to seek and save the lost, many of whom then turned around and demanded his death. Apparently, this is part of the cost we all have to pay for the freedom that the crucifixion death of Jesus purchased for us. God is real, but the enemy is too.

As I suspected, Pastor already knew about Lacey when I called him. He didn't really say much of anything to me or ask any questions. He didn't sound much like himself, which made me wonder about the merits of the marriage counseling he did with his wife. He sounded like Zoe Carter.

Chapter 29

Sampson's first night sleeping in his crib didn't really go well. The only way to get him to stop crying was to hold him. I had to take him downstairs so that he wouldn't wake up his sister. I dozed off and on throughout the night, sitting on the living room sofa in the dark with him in my arms. I wanted to shoot myself. I was very worried because I didn't see how this was going to work in the long run.

I woke again to the sound of the front door opening. Mama suddenly appeared wearing a thick winter coat and a knitted hat.

"Sam, what happened here?"

She had her hands on her hips. Her annoyance flared.

"I couldn't get him to sleep, so I…"

"What do you mean you couldn't get him to sleep," she questioned. "He's asleep now."

"Yes, but he doesn't stay asleep if I put him down."

"You are supposed to be in charge, not the baby!" she attacked.

"I know that, but…"

"He slept at the hospital, didn't he?" she argued. "Ain't nobody there had any problem getting him to sleep."

"Yes, but…"

"Don't tell me you were up all night!" she baited. "'Cause I know you got more sense than to do something like that."

I didn't respond. I knew her and feared for my life if I answered truthfully.

"Now see, this doesn't make any sense," she scolded. "That's why I decided to come and check on ya'll. Something told me you didn't know what to do with two. Give me the baby."

"What?"

"You heard me," she barked. "Go get now, cause you're getting on my nerves! I got the baby. You go and do what you got to do."

I did as I was told and turned and walked up the stairs. Carla was still asleep. Carly was, too. I slid back in bed and immediately fell asleep.

"Sam, where's Sampson?" Carla inquired.

"He's downstairs with Mama."

"How long has she been here?"

"Not long."

"Are you going to work?"

"I can barely move," I complained.

"Since your grandmother is here, do you mind if I take a quick shower before the other baby gets up?" she asked. "I'll only be a minute."

"No, go ahead."

"You have to listen for Carly."

"Okay."

It felt like I had just closed my eyes when Carla walked back into the room and woke me up. My whole body fought back hard when I first tried to get up. I somehow managed to make it to the shower, which was enough to restore most of my senses. But it still felt like I had been in a bar fight with some big dude… and lost.

Carla and Mama were sitting at the kitchen table, eating breakfast, when I came down. Carla was holding one of the babies in one arm and using the other hand to hold her fork.

"Where's the other one?" I wondered and looked around.

"He's upstairs in his crib," Carla replied.

"So now he wants to sleep!"

I poured myself a cup of coffee and sat down.

"That's not it," Mama interjected. "You just don't know what you're doing."

"Look, we're doing the best we can," I asserted.

"Listen to me now, both of you," Mama admonished. "Once he's been fed and you have changed his diaper, then lay him down in his crib on his back and don't pick him back up again."

"The nurse at the hospital told us not to put them on their stomachs because of their breathing," Carla said.

"I can't do that," I maintained. "He was crying so hard! I can't just let him cry for hours on end!"

"If he cries, you just touch and rub his little belly and talk to him sweet and gentle like," Mama instructed. "But whatever you do, don't pick him back up, no matter how much he fusses and cries. You might have to fight that battle for a couple of days, but sooner or later, he'll catch on. Babies ain't stupid."

"But if we let one cry, won't all the noise wake up the other one?" Carla wondered.

"No, not usually," she dismissed. "Babies don't need quiet to sleep. If they're tired enough, believe you me, they can sleep through a windstorm. Most people think that you have to tiptoe around them for them to sleep, but that's not the truth."

Carla and I just looked at each other. I was dazed and confused.

"I have been taking care of babies since I was nine years old," Mama presented. "I know what I'm talkin about."

We were motionless. She clearly saw the troubled looks on our faces.

"I think I should start coming over in the mornings to help ya'll a bit until you get the hang of everything," she offered.

"No, we couldn't ask you to do that," I replied.

"Nonsense," she expressed. "Did you forget? Them my babies too."

I looked at my wife again.

"Are you sure?" Carla asked.

"Yes, I'm sure," she indicated. "Gives me something meaningful to do."

"That would be a big help," Carla said, and her face lit up. "I'm honestly feeling a little anxious about everything."

"That's just normal," Mama replied. "But it won't take long for you to get the hang of it. It's like riding a bike. You'll see."

"I'm not so sure about that," Carla answered halfheartedly.

"No, it is," Mama encouraged. "You just got to trust yourself. You're the mama. You know best."

"Thanks, Mama," I said. "That would be a great relief

to both of us."

"And I'll stay out of your way too," Mama asserted. "I know it's your house and not mine. You don't need me up here imposing myself on everything."

"You don't have to worry about that," Carla quickly responded. "I enjoy your company. You're my mama too. Did *you* forget?"

Her words were like a shot straight to my heart and Mama's too. I held my breath for a few seconds.

"Thank you kindly," Mama said and choked up a little. "I feel the same way about you, sweetness. I surely do."

———— • ● • ————

Pastor Justin didn't reach out to me at all upon his return home from Oklahoma. I wasn't sure if I should call him. I didn't know where his head was at, and I was very concerned about crowding him.

If it were me, I would have had a lot of questions about what really happened with Lacey, but that's just me. He clearly wasn't overly interested in any of it any longer. Out of an abundance of caution, I decided to wait him out. Patience is a virtue.

It was several days before he called me. I'd say that he sounded a little better —less withdrawn. I tried to act normal, but it wasn't exactly feeling normal between us. I wondered if he resented me for something. After all, I'm a guy too, and he should be over his embarrassment about what happened with Lacey.

Basically, I just followed his lead, and he didn't ask anything about Lacey or what happened with the case. He reported only that they had a good trip and that he was glad that they had gone. It was a five-minute conversation.

The following Sunday was atypical. Although both Pastor Justin and Pastor Marlene were there, neither one of them gave the message. We had another guest speaker. It was a woman this time. Her name was Nancy Sullivan, and she was from the Albany area. Pastor Justin introduced her and said that they had known her for many years and that she was a close friend. She did a good job.

There was no mention of Lacey during the service. In fact, no one ever mentioned her name again, at least not from the pulpit. Our prayers for her had been answered, and we moved on like she never existed at all. We already had better singers.

However, I knew that something was still amiss with Pastor Justin. I could just tell. It was like he was merely going through the motions, like a lonely person at a birthday party graciously pretending to be happy.

A newspaper reporter called the church, looking for a comment from someone about Lacey. The caller was ultimately referred to me by Pastor Marlene. Needless to say, I had absolutely no interest in talking to any reporter. I reluctantly called her back.

"What can I do for you?" I asked directly.

"My name is Lisa Cantrell. I'm a freelance reporter, and I'm looking to write a story about what happened with Lacey Stanton."

"I see."

"I was hoping to get a comment from someone at her church about everything that happened with her."

"What kind of comment?" I asked. "Obviously, we are

glad that the police were able to locate her."

"Of course," she followed. "But her husband, Michael Stanton, is saying that the church played a big part in why she ended up leaving him in the first place."

"I don't believe that he ever attended our church," I replied. "How would he ever know that?"

"He said that the police brought in the pastors for questioning," she pressed. "Is that the case?"

"I think that they spoke to several people associated with the church because everybody there knows Lacey. We are a small congregation."

"Michael believes that Lacey was spreading lies about him at the church in order to get people to help her financially."

"What lies?" I questioned.

"He doesn't know for sure—something about him beating her and being abusive."

"Well, I'm sorry, but there is no way that anyone on staff can comment on anything about that," I asserted. "Lacey was a volunteer singer on our worship team. Her personal life is her own."

"So, you're telling me that Resurrection Life Church didn't help Lacey finance her escape from her marriage?"

"No, we didn't."

"Or help her to hide from her husband."

"No."

"Can I quote you on that?"

"Yes, you can quote me."

Chapter 30

Zoe decided to accept the settlement offer in her case. We made an appointment for her to come into the office the next day to sign the papers. She looked better— less bewildered. I also think she had maybe done something new with her hair.

She came bearing gifts. There were two medium-sized boxes. One had pink wrapping, and the other box was blue.

"What's that?" I asked as she sat down in the chair across from my desk.

"They're for you," she replied with a faint smile, and stood up again and handed them to me. "My mother told me that your wife just had twins. Congratulations!"

"Oh, you didn't have to do that," I said. "That's really thoughtful."

"I wanted to. You have been wonderful."

"Thank you so much."

"You're welcome."

"Here is the stipulation of settlement," I explained. "Before you sign it, do you have any questions?"

No, I don't think so."

"It's important that you remember that you cannot talk

about the terms of the settlement with anyone."

"I understand."

"We have to discontinue your case with the court. Once we get the stipulation of discontinuance filed, they will send me the check."

"Okay."

"And that will be that," I proclaimed. "I know that the money can't take away the pain that you went through, but hopefully this will give you some closure."

"Yes, I hope so too," she responded.

"So, please just sign your name at the mark... there."

She stood up again, leaned over the front of my desk, and signed the document.

She signed heavily as she sat back down.

"Um… my mother also told me what you did with them, and I wanted to thank you for that too."

"How are your parents?" I wondered.

"They're okay," she stated. "My dad was pretty angry at my mom for a while. But things have settled down a little, I guess. At least, they're talking."

"I hope you know that I was only trying to help," I explained. "I know that I took a big chance, possibly at your expense."

"No, it was good that you did," she said.

It was like there was an elephant in the middle of the room and both of them refused to see it," I reflected.

"It's been like that for a long time," she disclosed. "The problem is that I always felt caught in the middle between the two of them because the elephant was always staring back at me."

"That must have been really hard for you," I

sympathized. "I'm sorry."

"Thank you," she replied and bit her lower lip. "I don't really know if it's going to work out in the end with them. My mother only knows how to love me, and believe me, she's weird about that. She doesn't really know how to show it to her husband, or how to receive it. My dad stopped trying a long time ago, and she resents him for it."

"That's pretty insightful, I must say," I complimented.

"Not really," she refuted. "I've been watching it all happen up close and personal for forever."

"So, how are you really?" I wondered.

"I have a new counselor through the county who I really like. And I agreed to take this medication for depression."

"Good for you," I said. "I'm glad to hear it." "Like I said, I appreciate you trying to help me," she offered. "You didn't have to

go out of your way like that for me. I know that I haven't made it easy."

"I just want you to be happy," I expressed. "You deserve to be happy."

"I don't know about that," she answered and displayed a nervous half-smile.

She turned away.

"Life is hard, and love is often unkind," I spoke aloud to myself. "It's the

way of the world, Zoe."

"Ah, do you think I could ask you something else?"

"Yeah, sure," I answered. "What is it?"

"Do you think that a woman who has had... an *abortion*... can be forgiven by God?"

She looked desperate. Her eyes were twitching, and she

shivered.

"Why are you asking me?" I resisted.

She pointed to the bookcase behind me. On top was a small black and white

wooden cube with the words *"Amazing Grace"* written on the front.

"Someone gave me that when my mother died last year," I disclosed.

"Sorry to hear about your mother."

"Thank you."

"I saw it the first time I came here," she indicated. "And you asked me before if I believed in God. Remember?"

"Yes, I remember," I said. "I probably shouldn't be displaying that in the office. I honestly didn't think that anyone would ever notice it."

"I like it," she replied. "It's one of the reasons that I knew that I could trust you. Little things like that matter to me."

"Okay."

"I know that you're a good guy," she continued. "I just want to know what you think."

"Really?"

"Yeah, I think I do," she whispered.

"Um…since you asked," I spoke and hesitated briefly. "I don't believe that there is any sin that God can't forgive. The Bible says that where sin abounds, *grace* abounds much more."

"But even abortion?" she resisted. "My dad used to say that it was one of the mortal sins."

"Really?" I questioned. "Zoe, I'm not a Bible scholar by any stretch, but I'm pretty sure that nowhere in the Bible does it say that. Jesus certainly never said that. "

"Then why do people say that?" she questioned.

"I think that it's probably mostly politics," I suggested. "Abortions have existed throughout time. Yet the Bible is silent about it."

"But you think that abortion is a sin, right?"

"I don't think that abortion is God's will for us, if that's what you mean," I admitted. "But that's true for a lot of things, such as divorce or bigotry, both of which affect us greatly."

"I always thought it was in the Bible," she said. "This is all news to me."

"Honestly, I don't really know what to think either," I conceded. "But I have to say that I do know that children are one of God's greatest gifts – a real live miracle!"

"I believe that too," she professed. "That's the problem because…"

"Zoe, what's done is done," I pushed. "You were in a tough situation for sure, but another thing I know with absolute certainty is that nobody has the right to judge you. God loves you as much as He loves anybody?"

Shame washed over her, and she tensed her shoulders. Tears flooded her eyes, and she dabbed at them with a tissue.

"I don't think I believe that," she articulated. "I mean, how could He?"

"Because you are His daughter and the apple of His eye," I contended. "Trust me, I know what I'm talking about, now more than ever before."

"I want to believe you, but …"

"I have struggled with forgiveness myself," I interrupted.

"It almost choked the life out of me for real. I was slowly dying inside a little bit every day because I couldn't find it in my heart to forgive people who I thought had wronged me."

"It's really hard," she agreed.

"And the hardest person for me to forgive was me… for the things that I didn't like about myself and my relationships," I expressed.

She nodded her head and wiped at her eyes some more.

"Zoe, what I'm trying to say is you have to see your way through to forgiving yourself for whatever you think you did that was so wrong."

"But how do I do that exactly?" she pondered. "I feel dirty."

"Jesus once told a woman who asked a similar question to just move on from here and sin no more."

She sat straight up in her chair.

"He can make you clean inside and give you new life," I proclaimed. "If you put your faith in Him."

Her weeping eyes got big, and she slowly lowered her head. I sat perfectly still and opted to just let her cry it out. Truthfully, I ran out of words to say anyway. I felt inadequate.

Suddenly, a heaviness fell on us both like a thick California fog. My insides shivered even though I wasn't chilled. It was clear to me that God was doing something in her. So, I wisely waited on the Lord.

I don't know how long we sat there like that because I was caught up as well. The ringing phone brought me back to my senses. I had to answer it.

"I'm so sorry, but my next appointment has arrived," I

advised.

"Oh, I'm sorry," she said as she jumped to attention.

"No, not a problem," I asserted. "I hate that we have to end our time."

"Me too," she spoke. "I have never felt anything like that before."

"I think that God wants to heal you from the inside out?" I prophesied.

"You really think so?"

She scrunched her face. She didn't sound convinced.

"Zoe, there is a woman at my church whom I would like to connect you with. Her name is Becky Little, and she does most of our pastoral care. I think she might be a good resource to you. She can explain some things to you that I can't."

"Okay," she voiced.

"Good. I will reach out to her and give her your phone number. No pressure, but Becky is awesome, and she loves talking to young women."

"I'll do it if you say," she commented. "Honestly, I'm so tired of carrying these bad thoughts and feeling this way. I can't tell you how much this means to me. My head is still spinning."

Chapter 31

It was almost a week before I heard from Pastor Justin again. I felt bad. He just asked if we could meet. He was very direct and to the point. It was odd.

We met at our normal diner. It had been a while since I had been there— before Carla went into the hospital. I had missed the place like an old friend. I took a big whiff as soon as I walked in the door and exhaled.

Pastor was already there. He acknowledged me with just a quick nod of his head and looked away. He didn't wait for me to return the gesture. I took off my coat and sat down.

"What's up?" I asked.

"Not much," he replied. "How are you?"

"Good. I thought maybe you forgot about me."

"No, I didn't forget," he said. "I ordered your coffee."

"Then what gives?" I pressed. "I've been wondering."

"I have something to tell you," he muttered. "I haven't been looking forward to it."

"What is it?"

"Marlene and I have decided to move to Orlando."

"What?" I reacted.

"We are going to start over again," he claimed. "Her

parents have this huge house with five bedrooms and a pool. We can reset and wait on God."

"When?"

"Soon."

"Why?"

"Marlene never really liked it here with the weather and all, and it will be good for

the kids to be near their grandparents. They're not going to be here forever."

"But you hate the heat."

"I know," he conceded.

"Was this something that the counselor advised you to do?"

"Not exactly."

"Then I don't get it," I voiced.

"I have put my family through a lot."

"Not your fault," I asserted.

"Marlene doesn't agree with you."

"So you're going to make it up to her by moving to a place where you will be miserable?" I questioned.

He didn't really respond.

"This is something that God wants you to do?" I asked.

"I don't know what God wants from me anymore," he said. "I'm sorry, but I just don't know."

"Well, maybe you should wait on Him," I argued.

"That's what we are trying to do."

"By giving up?"

"We are not giving up," he resisted.

"What about the church?" I asked.

"We will work with the leadership team to find a new pastor."

"You know, this Lacey stuff will all blow over soon," I contended. "You don't think that you're overreacting?"

"We also spoke with our pastor in Ohio, Pastor Delaney," Pastor presented. "We have an incredible amount of respect for this man. He has been our pastor for almost 15 years. He married us. His opinion is that I needed to step down from ministry for a while."

"But why?"

"He said that I have been disqualified, and that I need time to be restored."

"*Disqualified?*" I repeated. "What a crock! Anybody can be a victim. Nobody knows that better than me."

"Sam, listen…"

"No, I'm trying to tell you that you didn't really do anything that wrong," I stressed. "It was all a trap. Lacey was out to entrap you from the very start."

"None of that matters!" he argued forcibly. "I don't want to ever have to think or hear about Lacey again! I'm not joking, I mean it!"

"Sounds to me like she's all you're thinking about," I submitted. "There's more to it than you know. She played you."

He shook his head..

"I let everybody down," he maintained. "Mostly, I let myself down."

"By being human?" I probed. "Nobody is perfect! Not even you! Did you really think that you were?"

"No, but it's important that the men and women of God walk worthy of the call."

"I don't know what that means," I replied in a dismissive manner.

"I know you don't."

"No, please don't talk down to me," I objected. "Please don't act like I lack the capacity to understand what's really going on here because I'm not a minister!"

"I didn't mean to belittle you in any way, Sam," Pastor responded. "I really didn't. But it is true that there is a mantle that those of us in the ministry carry that no one else can fully appreciate. It's… heavy at times."

"Doesn't change the fact that we are all only human and that we have an evil enemy who doesn't fight fair," I argued. "I know because I have had to fight hard against him."

"I know you have," Pastor conceded.

"Then what am I missing?"

"To whom much is given, much is required," he recited.

"Okay, but I don't believe for one second that this is something that you really want to do, or God is demanding you to do," I contended. "You love being our shepherd. I know you do!"

"Of course, I do, more than anything," he admitted. "I'm not one of those guys who claim that God is talking to them audibly all the time. But I do know for a fact that He wanted us to come here and pioneer this church. I know it in my inner knowing. And I'm convinced that He is pleased with the work that we have been doing here."

"Then what gives?" I begged. "Is God really that flakey that He would just change His mind at the drop of a hat?"

"It's not Him, it's me," he claimed. "I can't do it now…not the way that I am — not with this gigantic hole in my soul! Don't you see?"

"Then take a month off," I suggested. "Take whatever time you need to get yourself situated. Then come back and finish what you started."

"It doesn't work like that," Pastor maintained.

"Why not?"

"Sometimes we have to completely let go of something good in order to be positioned for something great," he preached. "It's a kind of pruning. It's the kingdom principle of seedtime and harvest. You've heard me teach it before."

"Well, yeah, but this is crazy!" I assailed.

"I'm sorry, Sam, but I have made up my mind."

"I see."

I shook my head. He turned away.

"I guess it's true, everyone leaves," I said.

"You know that's not true," he rose up. "You have outgrown that kind of victim mentality. It's beneath you now!"

"You're not the only one who doesn't know what to believe anymore," I set forth.

"Listen, I know that this comes as a big surprise to you and that you are upset, but please look at this with your *spiritual eyes*, and not with your *broken heart*."

I turned away and took a sip of my coffee, which was lukewarm. Usually, I could drink it that way with no problem, but I pushed the cup away. A sea of emotion was tossing and turning within me, making me feel sick to my stomach.

"I owe this to my wife," he maintained. "You would do it for yours. For Carla, you would do it too. I saw you completely let go of everything for her, even your children."

I flinched and did a double-take.

"Sam, I need you to support me in this, even if you don't agree."

"I honestly don't know if I can," I acknowledged.
"You have to because I don't think that I can do this without
you," Pastor claimed. "In many ways, you are my only
friend. I could barely hold my head up on Sunday. I felt all
alone without you."

I swallowed hard.

"How soon is soon?" I asked.

"A couple of months. We have to get the house ready to
sell and get the boys through this grading period in school."

I knew that he was right about everything, but I refused
to concede anything in that moment. I needed time to fully
digest this turn of events and to sulk. Lacey's little schemes
worked perfectly, and she brought down our whole church,
at least temporarily, in the process. It was hard for me not to
see this as anything but a victory for the kingdom of
darkness.

———————•●•———————

I knew that I had to tell Carla something, so I just told
her that the pastors had decided to move to Orlando to be
closer to family. I felt that I couldn't tell her that the move
had anything to do with Lacey."

"Aww, I'm really going to miss them," Carla said.
"She's so nice. I wonder what is making them make such a
drastic decision?"

"I'm not happy about it," I complained.

"You didn't tell him that, did you?"

"Yeah, kinda," I sheepishly admitted.

"Sam, I'm sure that it was a hard decision for them to
make," she pointed out. "What did he say?"

"That he needed to do it for his family."

"I think that you just have to accept that if you're really his friend," she urged.

"I just feel that he's making a mistake," I answered. "In fact, I know he is."

"Honey, you know I love you with my whole heart, but sometimes you are too hard on people. You have certain *expectations* that nobody can possibly live up to."

"Do you think I do that to you?" I wondered.

"Honestly, sometimes," she indicated. "But I'm not talking about me. You have to give the people in your life permission to be wrong, and that's okay."

"I have to accept it anyway," I concluded. "He's a grown man. He can do whatever he wants."

"You are, too, and you can make yourself support your friend."

"All true," I relented.

"Aw, come on, you can do this," she encouraged. "I know it probably feels like you're losing your only friend. But I know you, and you'll probably meet some other cool kid tomorrow during recess."

"Not helpful," I said with a half-smile.

"I have no idea what the two of you talk about anyway," she goaded. "Neither one of you likes sports, and I know you guys don't talk about your feelings. So what else is there?"

"You'd be surprised."

"You mean bored."

"We both like girls."

"So it's like that?" she asked. "Really?"

"I cannot confirm nor deny," I played along. "We're blood brothers."

"Keep your old boring secrets," she replied. "Just remember, two can play that game."

"Gotcha."

"When are they going to leave?" she wondered.

"In two months."

"Whoa, there's going to be a lot of sad people," she lamented.

"Yeah, I know."

"Technically, he is my first and only pastor," I voiced.

"Mine too."

———— • ● • ————

I didn't sleep much again. This time, it wasn't a hungry baby who needed to be fed and changed that was keeping me up. It was like my brain just wouldn't quiet down enough to let me rest. My thoughts were all over the place, running away with me.

I called Pastor Justin first thing the next morning.

"Hi, how are you?" I asked.

"Good."

"I'm sorry," I spoke.

"It's all good, Sam."

"No, I've been thinking about it all night," I divulged. "I should have been more supportive. It's not an excuse, but I was hurt."

"I know."

"Other people will be too," I pointed out.

"I know that too… But Jesus had his favorite disciples. It was different between them."

"Okay... I got you," I vowed.

"Thanks, Sam. This means more to me than you know."

"Forget about it," I breathed. "It's the least I can do."

Chapter 32

Pastor Marlene gave the Sunday message. Just prior to that, Pastor Justin made an appeal to the congregation to come to "a *family meeting*" on the following Thursday night. He just said that it was important, and he was asking everyone who loved our church to come out. I was sad already.

Mama agreed to stay with the babies so that Carla could go to the meeting. We were both silent in the car. It felt like I was going to another funeral. Carla touched me on my thigh, and I looked at her and quickly raised both eyebrows. She gave me a reassuring smile.

There were about a hundred people there, a remarkable turnout for us on such short notice. However, some people apparently couldn't get a babysitter because there were a dozen little kids running around. Carla and I sat in the second row. I wanted Pastor Justin to be able to see me. The overall mood of the crowd was upbeat, almost festive. Clearly, most people had no idea what this was all about.

There were audible gasps throughout the sanctuary when Pastor Justin, standing behind the podium with Pastor Marlene, announced that they were resigning as senior pastors. His words echoed throughout from person to person. He just said that they had prayed about it and felt that the Lord wanted them to make this move now. He further advised that the search for a new pastor was underway, and that there were several pastors interested in taking over.

Pastor Marlene got emotional when she told everyone that this was a particularly hard decision for them because they had grown so close to everyone over the last nine years. She said that this was the only home her children ever knew.

"I just want to personally thank each and every one of you for opening your hearts to my family and me," she offered. "It has been one of the greatest honors of my life to have been your pastor."

A hush fell like a blanket, and the air was thick with shock, sadness, and grief. I peered over at Carla and saw that she was crying.

"I don't really understand," a woman shouted from her seat. "It feels like you guys are being stolen away from us. We just went through that with Lacey. Why would God do this?"

"I can't answer that," Pastor Justin replied. "His thoughts are so much higher than ours. But I do know that He is faithful and that He has a plan to finish what He has started in you and in this church. Your hope was never in Pastor Marlene or me, it has to be in the Lord. We are just His vessels."

Another woman jumped to her feet.

"I just want to thank you both for everything that you have done for my family and me. I don't know what I would have done this past year with everything that is going on with me and my health if it weren't for you. Pastor Marlene, I think of you as the sister that I never had. My heart is broken that you are leaving and… sorry."

She plopped down in her seat and turned into a pile of mush.

"I hope that you know that we love this church," Pastor Justin said. "There is no group of people and no place on earth where I would rather pastor. I mean that sincerely."

"Is there a chance that you could come back, say, after a year or so?" a man asked from his seat."

"At this point, we don't know what God has next for us, so I can't answer that either," Pastor Justin replied. "But we are open to whatever it is that He has for us to do."

"I just want to say that I love you," Taylor, a young boy of about six, cried out.

He then turned to his mother and collapsed in her arms. His feeble cries filled the room, and joined by just about everybody else's, sounded like the soundtrack to the saddest of tales. Nobody was moving about, not even the children. Most people looked shell-shocked.

The meeting lasted for two grueling hours. To their credit, the pastors let everyone who wanted to say something speak. For the most part, everyone was respectful and considerate. But it was extremely hard to listen to people's trauma dump and bleed aloud from their souls. I can't imagine how the pastors must have felt standing there.

It was a major relief when it was finally over. Immediately, a small group converged around the pastors. I quickly poked my head in and advised Pastor Justin that we had to get home to the babies and that we would talk later. He nodded his head.

"Ah, Sam, could I just have a quick moment before you

leave?" Pastor Marlene asked and gestured toward their offices.

"Oh, sure," I answered.

I told Carla that I needed a minute and followed Pastor Marlene to her office. She opened the door and let me walk in first. She closed the door behind us. I had never been in her office before. It was just a little smaller than Pastor Justin's office.

"Have a seat," she directed.

She sat behind the desk.

"Well, that was painful!" she expressed. "Worse than I imagined it would be."

"Yes, it was."

"It was all I could do not to run out of there crying my eyes out," she revealed. "My knees were shaking the whole time."

"I thought you handled it well," I maintained. "You both did."

"Thank you for saying that," she remarked. "I think I have a tension headache."

"You should probably go home and put your feet up," I suggested.

"Trust me, I will," she indicated. "But I just wanted to thank you for everything that you have done for us. You have been great, really great. I don't know what we would have done without you."

"It was nothing," I said.

"Justin doesn't have a lot of friends outside of the ministry," she explained. "It's easy to lose yourself completely when your whole life is dealing with other people's problems. Not surprisingly, people come to us with everything, not just spiritual matters."

"I know they do."

"We need an outlet too, where we can just be ourselves and not have to worry about being judged or preached to. You have given Justin that. So, I'm grateful to you for that too."

"I get it," I affirmed. "I know it's not quite the same, but lawyering is all about other people's problems too."

"No, I can see that, especially now with everything that happened with the state police," she contended. "It was a nightmare for us. You were our saving grace."

"Well, I should probably be thanking you too for your part in taking care of Lacey."

"Huh, what do you mean?" she questioned.

She shoved her hair away from her face.

"How much did you pay her?" I asked.

She jolted upright. Her expression closed up.

"Who said I paid her anything?" she challenged.

I went poker-faced.

The standoff lasted for several extended seconds. A muscle in her jaw twitched.

"Doesn't matter," she finally said, and her expression hardened. "I would have paid more."

"So, you knew the entire time where Lacey was?" I questioned.

"I had no idea where she was," she refuted. "I gave her twenty-four hours to pack up her stuff and get out of town. I didn't care where she went, and I certainly didn't tell her to make it look like she was kidnapped and murdered."

"Does Pastor Justin know?"

"No, he doesn't."

"I didn't think so."

"And if you're really his friend, you won't tell him," she asserted.

"So that's really why we are having this conversation now," I said. "You figured that I knew about the money, and you just want to make sure that I don't tell Pastor."

"I didn't do anything illegal," she reasoned.

"You lied under oath to law enforcement," I charged. "That's a crime."

"I told you before, I'd do anything to protect my family."

"Even lying to the police and to your lawyer?"

"Yes."

"And to your husband?"

"I never lied to Justin."

"What do you mean you never lied to him?" I refuted. "You went all that way to Oklahoma to go to counseling to supposedly work on your marriage, and you sat there and said nothing."

A flush crept up her face.

"I know him, and this is something that he definitely would want to know," I contended.

"I never wanted to move up here in the first place," she argued. "I only agreed because Justin wanted it so badly. But he never would have met that Jezebel if we hadn't moved to this Godforsaken place."

"There are bad people in Florida, too."

"Believe me, not like this one," she disparaged. "You should have heard the things she said to me."

"It was all a trap to get money," I reported. "Lacey was never really interested in Pastor romantically, or vice versa.

She was just a project to him."

"I couldn't take that chance," she said. "I didn't know what kind of game she was playing."

"It sounds to me like you have a little game in you, too," I asserted.

"That's ridiculous!" she exclaimed with a roll of her eyes. "I just fought back against a witch."

"Then tell Pastor what you did!"

Her eyes got big.

"I can't do that," she admitted.

"Because you leveraged your husband's guilt to get what you wanted from him," I condemned.

"That's not the way I see it," she resisted.

"Did you not listen to anything he just said out there? You couldn't feel his pain?"

"We'll find another church," she submitted. "Everybody loves Justin. Who wouldn't? He's perfect. You love him, too. That's why you won't tell him."

"Sounds to me like you've got it all figured out," I criticized.

"Sam, you have it all wrong," she maintained. "You're making me out to be this bad person, but I would never do anything to hurt Justin. He's been my whole world since the first moment that I ever laid eyes on him, from our very first kiss. This makes perfect sense for us. Don't you see?"

"No, I don't," I disputed. "He's literally drowning in shame and guilt because he thinks that he broke his vows to God and to you. It could be years before he gets over something that you know in your heart isn't really true at all."

"Please, I'm begging you to just let sleeping dogs lie,"

she advocated. "Absolutely nothing good can come out of telling him."

"Ah, I don't know about that, but fortunately for you, it's also true that Pastor Justin isn't really interested in hearing anything else from me about what happened with Lacey," I advised.

"So, you won't tell him?" she implored.

"Not if he doesn't ask me directly."

"I don't know what to say," she exclaimed and slowly exhaled.

"What else is there to say?" I asked sarcastically. "Looks like you both win— you and Lacey, the dynamic duo. I hope you're happy."

She lowered her head and fiddled with her earring.

"I'm sorry, Sam. I really am," she spoke. "But for what it's worth, I can't thank you enough."

"Please don't thank me," I insisted. "It makes me feel like an accomplice to something unholy."

Chapter 33

The pastors found a buyer for their house in less than a week. Apparently, a lot of people were interested in it because it was located so close to the elementary school. They actually got more than their asking price. With this major hurdle gone, they were able to move ahead with their plans to relocate without undue delay.

A search committee was put together to find candidates for the job of Pastor. Although Pastor Justin felt strongly that I should be on the committee, I declined the offer. I didn't want to say anything to him, but I wasn't 100% sure that Carla and I were staying at the church after he was gone. While we had no specific plans to go anywhere, I felt that it made sense to leave the option open.

There must have been at least ten going-away parties for them. It seemed that every group in the church wanted to say goodbye in its own way. I went to most of them just to support Pastor Justin. Needless to say, I was present in body only as my heart was definitely not in the festivities.

Carla was right, Pastor Justin and I never really talked that much about our feelings when we were together. We were content to enjoy each other's company without jumping into the deep end all of the time. I preferred not to process any of my feelings about his move in real time, and he didn't want to have to talk about leaving the church or Lacey with me. It wasn't avoidance exactly. Unlike most women, men tend to recharge best when we completely power down first. God made us that way.

We got together several times before he left. We laughed and joked together like always. We promised to stay in touch, but I wasn't sure how much of that was really in the cards for us. Time passes, life happens, and people change. I got it. That's the reason why it's so important to appreciate the good times when they happen, because they don't always last.

"Sam, can I tell you something?" Pastor asked.

"Sure."

"I never had a Black friend before," he confessed. "Growing up in a small town in Ohio, there really wasn't much mixing of the races. I went to an all-boys high school, and there was only one Black kid in my class. I always regretted that I didn't really know him."

"Really? Why was that?"

"I don't really know," he contemplated. "I always noticed him, and he seemed nice. I was curious about him, is all."

"Are you saying that because you met me, you're no longer curious? Is that it?"

"No, that's not it at all."

"Then what?" I exacted.

"Because of you, I regret not knowing him even more. I think I might have really missed out on a divine relationship with a brother at a time when I really could have used one."

"Hmm, look at it this way, you got a do-over," I jokingly remarked. "With an even better model."

"Yes, yes, I certainly did," he said under his breath. "God is faithful."

Just as I assumed, as soon as Carla got over her initial apprehension about motherhood, she quickly found her footing, and she took to it like a fish to water. After a couple of weeks, we didn't need Mama to come over every day. She became our babysitter instead, which worked out best for Mama, too, because Carla was very particular about how she wanted the babies cared for, and Mama was so opinionated. They were bound to clash at some point if they were together too much, and, trust me, nobody wanted to witness that. Between the two of them, I pretty much just did as I was told.

I tried to give Carla a break as much as I could. She was tired most evenings, so I did a lot of the late-night duties, which I honestly grew to cherish because those moments became my special time with the babies. I liked holding them and talking to them about the state of the world and, of course, about Jesus, the Savior. I'm pretty sure that they understood every word I said, too, by the way they listened so intently to me- a father just knows these things.

Sometimes I just held them and sang and prayed aloud over them. The love that I felt for my children was like nothing I ever felt before. It was an all-consuming fire that warmed my heart and comforted my soul through and through, down to my toes.

I couldn't help but equate the feeling to the kind of love that the Father God must have for us, His children—although admittedly His love is much greater. Undoubtedly, this is the reason why we can't possibly love each other enough or too much.

This realization shook me to my core and settled into the crevices of my soul like sweet butter on dry toast. I knew that there was no such thing as heaven on earth... but these times were close enough for me… for now.

"What are you doing?"

"What?" I asked and jumped to attention from a light sleep.

"Put her in her crib and come to bed," Carla directed. "There is something else that I need you to do."

I had no idea how long I had been asleep in the rocking chair in the nursery. I put Carly down and checked on Sampson one more time. He was soaking wet, so I quickly changed him again before I turned down the light and walked out of the room. I was still groggy and operating mostly on autopilot.

Carla had the light on in our room, and she was sitting up on the side of the bed facing me with her legs crossed at the knees and one foot on the floor.

"What are you doing?" I questioned.

She pointed to her foot.

"Can you take my socks off?" she asked.

"Is something wrong with your leg?"

"No, I just need help."

"I went down on one knee and began taking off the sock on the foot that was dangling in front of me."

I caught my breath at the sight of her glossy, *passion red* toenails that shone with a shimmering brilliance. New passions began to stir in me, and I leered at her.

"I thought that maybe …you might like to … *adore* me," she said and threw her head back seductively.

• ● •

All spiritually mature Christians want to be used by God for the upbuilding of His kingdom. After all, this is something that we have been specifically commissioned to do. The problem is that *"being used"* typically hurts— sometimes it hurts a lot. And at the same time, the whole world is watching and judging. Accordingly, as true believers, we must all learn to overcome our own personal challenges the way that light drowns out the darkness.

Indeed, all of the champions of faith in the Bible had hard lives with plenty of pain and opposition— including Moses, David, the disciples, and Paul. We were all conceived in sin, born in a woman's pain, and saved and kept by our faith in the shed blood of an innocent man. These are the ties that bind us together as children of God.

Inevitably, bad things will happen in our lives that we cannot possibly predict, prevent, or fathom. But we still must take them in stride and march on, with our heads held high, toward an assured victory. This is an important part of guarding our overall witness to the world.

Heaven is a beautiful promise for believers to hope for and cling to, but it's not the ultimate goal. It's really about learning to love and trust God in both the good and the bad times, which is its own reward because there is truly nothing better than loving and being loved by Him. In the end, everything else pales in comparison.

Ed Thompson is a lay minister in Syracuse, New York. He is also a trial attorney in New York, having practiced law in Syracuse for more than twenty-five years. He is a former federal prosecutor and a former assistant public defender. Additionally, Ed received a master's degree in biblical studies from Alliance Theological Seminary in 2020. Previously, Ed received a BA degree from Ohio Northern University in 1982 and a JD Degree from Albany Law School in 1985. He is the author of four legal fiction titles, including Cursed Black. Presently, he resides in Baldwinsville, New York, with his wife and daughter.